'Billy, m.. yesterday:

...........pens in this game.

....'You'll miss,' I said.

.... wiped his nose on his sleeve. 'Loser,' he sneered

....ran for the kick-off.

.... hurt. That really hurt. I'd always given two

....dred per cent and he knew it. But maybe he was

........erhaps I was a loser. Whichever way you looked

....d totally messed up. And not just with the team.

....here, right at the back of all this, I felt bad

....e I'd lost a good mate too. Me and Billy had been

........than knotted string once. It made me wonder

........ch was better: staying friends with someone or

stay..ng in the Cup?

I ...ooched towards a corner flag, head bent low,

....d. so deep inside my pockets they could have been

....rching for black holes in space. That was why I

.... see Mandy at first. I heard Mr Crozier greet the

....shloe teacher, looked along the touchline – and there

....e was . . .

CHRIS d'LACEY

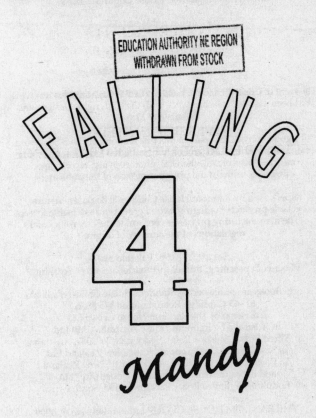

FALLING
4
Mandy

CORGI BOOKS

FALLING FOR MANDY
A CORGI BOOK : 0552 548669

Published in Great Britain by Corgi Books,
an imprint of Random House Children's Books

This edition published 2003

1 3 5 7 9 10 8 6 4 2

Papers used by Random House Children's Books are natural,
recyclable products made from wood grown in sustainable forests.
The manufacturing processes conform to the environmental
regulations of the country of origin.

Set in 12/15.5pt Palatino by
Phoenix Typesetting, Burley-in-Wharfedale, West Yorkshire

Corgi Books are published by Random House Children's Books,
61–63 Uxbridge Road, London W5 5SA,
a division of The Random House Group Ltd,
in Australia by Random House Australia (Pty) Ltd,
20 Alfred Street, Milsons Point, Sydney, NSW 2061, Australia,
in New Zealand by Random House New Zealand Ltd,
18 Poland Road, Glenfield, Auckland 10, New Zealand
and in South Africa by Random House (Pty) Ltd,
Endulini, 5a Jubilee Road, Parktown 2193, South Africa

THE RANDOM HOUSE GROUP Limited Reg. No. 954009
www.kidsatrandomhouse.co.uk

A CIP catalogue record for this book is available
from the British Library.

Printed and bound in Great Britain by
Bookmarque Ltd, Croydon, Surrey

for Jane Burnard,
who was there at the kick-off

I would also like to thank David Fickling
and Liz Cross for spirited team talk
and touchline guidance

Sometimes it's a funny old game

This is a sort of . . . love story – sorry. I know, it makes me shudder as well. It's about me, Danny Miller, and this girl called Mandy, though she doesn't come into it for ages yet. I s'pose it's a football story, too, 'cos that's what brought us, y'know, *together*. It kind of begins in the sixty-fifth minute of our second-round cup tie against Durrington Grange. But if we started there you wouldn't get to hear about Billy's tongue. And that is something worth hearing about.

The tongue was all to do with Marcia Williams. She's the 'other girl' in this story. Marcia is in the year above ours. She's got ash-blonde hair, big green eyes and 'legs that look as if they ought to be on stilts'. That's what Mr Crozier, our games teacher, says. He takes us for footie. He knows about legs.

Scott Newton was the one who started it. We were clawing our way past the netball courts, pretending to be swapping football cards, when Scotty said, 'Nine – her hair's a nine.'

'Eight,' said Billy, dragging his fingers along the mesh.

Ffion Griffiths (yellow bib, wing defence) heard the rattle. She looked up and glared.

Scott said loudly, 'Zinedine Zidane's a weird name, isn't it? Who wants to swap him for Michael Owen?'

We shuffled our cards. Ffion melted back to her game.

'I agree with Scott,' I hissed. 'Her hair's dead nice. Definitely nine.'

'What about her bum, then?' Billy asked.

Scott shrugged. 'Bums can't be nicer than hair, can they?'

I kneeled down and risked a glance. Marcia (yellow bib, goal shooter) leaped for the ball as it sailed out of play. Her skirt flapped open, but it didn't lift. 'No,' I reported.

We settled on six for her bum.

'Legs,' said Scott. 'They've gotta be good.'

'Eight,' said Billy.

'And a half,' Scott added.

We took another look. Marcia had her back to us, cocking a hip.

'Yep,' I said and stuck up a thumb, just as a voice said, 'Danny, what you doing?'

'Aw, no. What's *she* doing here?' growled Billy.

'She' was my younger sister, Alice. She went to the junior school next door. I was supposed to be walking her home that night. She should have been waiting for me at the gates.

'Go away,' said Billy. 'We're busy. Tell her, Danny.'

Alice glanced at the netball players. She sussed our game in a flash. 'They're giving you scores if they fancy you!' she shouted.

I clamped a chewing-gummed hand around Alice's gob. She kicked and bucked, but the damage was done. The game immediately ground to a halt. Kym Casey (red bib, goal defence) turned towards us and frowned. Billy, stupidly, blew her a kiss.

'In your dreams, ape boy,' Kym hit back. She stuck out a pimple of tongue.

Bad news. Billy went ape. Not only did he cling like a chimp to the mesh, he rolled out a tongue like a piece of carpet. 'Ooh, ooh – urk,' he grunted.

'*Urk?*' went Scott. 'That doesn't sound right.'

It wasn't. Billy was pinned to the mesh – by his tongue. Somehow, he'd wedged it into a hole.

Kym Casey screeched with laughter. The girls grouped up and wandered over. Marcia, who had come to the front of the group, folded her arms and sighed at Billy. 'That is disgusting,' she said.

'Obviously a perv,' said a girl at the edge.

'He's stuck. Help us get him out,' I begged, as Alice bit my hand and freed herself.

Ffion stepped up, licking her lips. She tossed a netball from palm to palm. 'I'll get him out,' she said.

'What you doing?' yelped Scott as Ffion took aim.

'Goal shooting,' she said, tilting the ball at Billy's face.

'Yeah, go for it,' said Alice, scowling fit to bust.

'Urk,' went Billy, desperately trying to force the mesh wider.

I decided to appeal on sporting grounds. 'He's our striker!' I cried. 'Don't injure him, please! We're playing Durrington in the Cup tomorrow. He's good in the air. Don't hurt his head!'

Ffion paused and consulted Marcia. 'Does a striker need a willy?'

Marcia rolled her eyes.

'Thought not,' said Ffion, and hurled the ball straight at Billy's groin.

At the moment the ball made contact, he catapulted backwards onto the grass. One hand shot to his stupid mouth, the other to his . . . important little place.

Alice, unrepetent, leaned over him and stormed, 'I hope it hurts all night!'

Ffion licked her finger and ticked the air. Marcia and the netballers drifted away.

'Billy, are you all right?' I asked. I kneeled beside him and touched his shoulder. He was writhing on the ground as if he'd been pole-axed.

'It's only his willy,' said Scott. 'It's only like being in the wall at a free kick and forgetting to cover yourself . . . down there.'

'He's acting,' sneered Alice. 'Looking for sympathy.'

'Shut up,' I said. 'What would you know?'

'I'm in our Christmas play,' she said. 'I know about acting. I'm an angel. So there.' She kicked Billy's leg and he sat up shouting, 'Bog off, shortie!'

Alice showed him her angelic tongue. Billy sneered back at her and spat on the ground.

'You sure you're all right?' I asked.

He sighed and jumped to his feet, unhurt. ''Course,' he sniffed and glared at Alice.

We *all* glared at Alice.

'Lads: always trying it on,' she said.

'She's mental,' said Scott, and I nodded in agreement.

If only I'd known, then, about feminine intuition.

FIRST HALF

CHAPTER 1

So there we were in our game against Durrington: one–nil down in the sixty-fifth minute, looking set to go out of the Inter-Schools Cup.

'Long ball game!' Mr Crozier was bellowing. 'No time for anything fancy now!'

But it was something fancy that won us the match.

Despite the slim margin, Durrington weren't sitting on the game at all. I was constantly having to funnel back deep to cover their overlaps down the right. But on one attack their winger tried to take me on and ended up stumbling over the ball. I took possession and quickly switched the play out of our area. We suddenly had a chance to hit them on the break.

'Hoof it, Danny!' Mr Crozier screamed.

I looked up, saw Billy in a few feet of space and whacked the ball over the Durrington back four. Billy slipped his marker – and the scramble was on.

'Good ball!' Mr Crozier clapped. 'Come on, Peters! Run for it, you rhubarb!'

Everybody knows that Billy isn't the fastest stick of rhubarb in the world, but he reached the ball first and even managed to carry it into their box. But somehow, it wouldn't sit up for a shot. Two Durrington defenders closed him down, forcing him to swerve away from goal. They were poking at his heels, trying to win the ball back, when suddenly . . .

'Owww!'

Billy went down with a yelp of pain. He tumbled over, feeling his back as if someone had punched him hard in the kidneys. The ball rolled clear. One worried defender booted it away. The other spread his hands and looked at Billy as if to say, 'What? What did I do?'

PENALTY?!

The word seemed to leap out of every puddle. The ref took a long hard look at Billy, turned on his heels . . . and pointed to the spot.

I don't miss penalty kicks. Ever since I was six years old and Dad painted some goalposts and a shark-toothed goalie on the doors of our garage, I've been putting spot-kicks away with ease. This one was no exception. The Durrington goalie was springing about like a chimpanzee as I set the ball down on my favourite blob of paint. He could have swung off the crossbar for all I cared, it wouldn't have made a scrap of difference. He was still blowing onto his gloves for luck when my shot whizzed past him and hit the net. Willowbrook hands reached up to the sky. Shoulders dropped on the Durrington side. They had held the lead since the third minute of the game – and were about to chuck it away completely.

Right from the kick-off, Scott won possession and lashed the ball high into their half again. The same defender who had given away the penalty chested the ball down neatly enough, but then panicked and sent a suicidal pass across the face of goal. Billy swooped and hit a first-time shot. It skimmed across the goalmouth, in off a post. There was no way back for Durrington after that. We were in the third round of the Inter-Schools Cup. And like everyone else, I was ecstatic.

But on the trek back to the changing rooms I overheard the Durrington centre-back wailing: 'I

never touched that striker. He dived. He's a cheat!'
And I nearly turned round and fisted him one. But
you can get yourself booked even off the pitch and
anyway, I sort of *agreed* with him.

I mean, who in their right mind punches an
opponent, *in the penalty area*, when you're one–nil
up in a crucial cup tie, and you've only got minutes
to go? It didn't make sense. At the time, when the
referee had pointed to the spot, all I could think of
was grabbing the ball and firing Willowbrook
back into the match. But while we were getting
stripped for the showers, I looked at Billy's back
for signs of a bruise. There was nothing. Not even
a reddish mark. He had definitely faked that foul.

Mr Crozier knew it too. 'Good game, lads.
Fighting performance. Keep this up and you might
be on for the medals – or in your case, Peters, an
Oscar, perhaps.'

'Eh?' said Billy, towelling his hair.

Mr Crozier threw him a sideways glance. 'It's
what they give to film stars for acting, boyo.' He
yowled with pain and rubbed his back. The whole
team whooped with laughter.

'Don't get it,' said Billy, acting the innocent.

'"Don't get it,"' Mr Crozier repeated scornfully.
'You'll be giving diving lessons to the park
ducks next.'

Which is how Billy earned his nickname 'Quack'.

From that day on, every time Billy hit the deck in a game, somebody made a quacking sound. Everybody laughed off his diving 'act'. It was part and parcel of the game, they said.

CHAPTER 2

But on the way home that night, I couldn't stop myself asking Billy about it: 'Why'd you do it?' I said.

'Do what?' he sniffed.

'Billy, don't mess with me,' I tutted. 'You can get a yellow card for diving, you know. You're gonna be in trouble if you do it too often.'

He swapped his bag to the opposite shoulder. 'Nah, that's one of the tricks,' he grinned. He drew me over to a low brick wall, unzipped his bag, and pulled out a tatty-looking video cassette.

'*Strike Hard*?' I said, wrinkling my nose. On the front was a picture of a footballer making a sliding tackle and his agonized opponent buckling at the knee.

'Read this,' said Billy. He turned the box over.

Now *you* can be the all-round super striker! Learn the tricks the professionals use to gain vital extra seconds in front of goal! Discover the best moment to tug an opponent's shirt . . . Learn how to deal with man-to-man marking . . . Watch the A-to-Z guide to winning free kicks. Top tips by top players. Strike HARD, Strike MEAN. And above all, STRIKE!

I shoved it back into his chest. 'That's rubbish. Where'd you get it?'

'Careful,' he cried as the box flipped open. 'I bought it off this bloke at a car boot sale.'

'Aw, Billy!'

'What?'

'Top players wouldn't make a video like that. Who's on it?'

'Dunno,' he said, checking the box over. 'Some bloke called Damien Clegge.'

'Who did *he* play for?'

'Don't think it says.'

I swung my kit bag onto my shoulder and started back up the road in disgust.

'That kidney punch I tried this afternoon,' Billy

clamoured. 'It comes under "K" in the A-to-Z of winning free kicks. Good, isn't it?'

'It's cheating. Get rid of it.'

'You're joking. It cost me ten ninety-nine. That's nearly two weeks' paper money.'

'It'll cost a lot more than that, you moron, if Crozzy or a referee catches you at it.'

He gave me a supercilious grin. 'Tells you not to worry about the ref,' he prattled. 'You just have to know where he is, that's all.' He pointed to a lamp-post. 'Say that's him, and you're the defender. All I have to do is stay this side of you. That way the ref can't see me very well. Then when I fall he's not sure what's happened – and the striker always gets the benefit of the doubt. That's what Damien says. Look, I'll show you—'

'Get off!' I shouted, pushing him away.

'Whassamatter?' he sneered.

I wasn't sure I knew. I'd felt dead twitchy since the end of the game. Something was definitely making me boil. Something more than Damien Clegge and his stupid A-to-Z of winning free kicks. I just couldn't work out what it was right then. So I blurted: 'You're stupid. Leave me alone!'

'No problem,' he snapped. And we drifted to opposite sides of the pavement. We had gone a few strides when he spat out bitterly: 'Loads of Premier League players dive.'

'Get lost,' I muttered.

'You get lost.'

'Yeah?'

'Yeah!'

And I kicked a pebble off the pavement – and went.

CHAPTER
3

A few minutes later I barged through our back gate, leaving it banging on its hinges. Bigfoot, our rabbit, flattened his ears and wisely hopped back to the safety of his hide (he'd seen me in one of my moods before). In the kitchen, Alice was doing her homework. Dad was in the front room, watching the news. Mum was digging about in the freezer. I slung my bag against the base of a cupboard and sank down into an empty chair.

Mum looked up and closed the freezer door. 'Oh dear. Do I take it we lost?'

'No,' I snapped, flicking pencil shavings at a smirking Alice. 'Won, two–one. I scored a penalty.'

'Well done,' said Mum. 'So why Mr Grumpy?'

I stretched out my feet as far as they would go. Millie, our cat, miaowed and leaped over them. 'Nothing. What's for tea?'

Mum moved across the room and switched on the kettle. 'That's a very glum look for "nothing", Danny. Come on, what's bothering you?'

'Girls,' said Alice. 'He's at that age.'

'You get on with your drawing,' said Mum.

But as usual, Alice wouldn't give up. 'I'm right,' she fluted with a flick of her ponytail. 'I saw him and Scott Newton and Billy Peters watching netball after school the other night. They were giving Marcia Williams marks out of ten.'

My face turned horribly red.

'Marcia Williams?' said Mum. 'Do I know this girl?'

'She's in Year Nine,' Alice continued. 'She's got long blonde hair and a cutesy nose. He gave her legs an eight and a— Ow!'

'Danny! Don't kick your sister,' Mum scolded.

'What's going on?' Dad shouted from the front.

'Just Alice,' Mum called, 'giving sisterly advice.'

'Oh,' Dad grunted. He was used to Alice giving everyone advice.

Alice turned down her sock and rubbed the bone. 'You're for it,' she hissed. 'That hurt, that did.' She pushed her snub nose into my face. 'You

fancy Marcia Williams. And I'm going to *tell* her!'
She snatched up her things and hurtled away.

There was a long, embarrassing pause.

'Fish fingers, all right?' Mum said eventually.
She waved a box as if in surrender. Millie jumped
on a stool and miaowed like mad.

'I'm going to my room,' I sulked. 'And if Billy
flipping Peters rings up this weekend, tell him to
just stuff off, OK?' I stomped to the door, pushing
past Dad as he came into the kitchen.

'What's with him?' I heard him ask Mum.

'Well,' she replied with a weary sigh, 'if tell-tale
Alice is to be believed, it appears that half Danny's
class have an adolescent crush on a netball star
called Marcia Williams. I think he's had a fall-out
with Billy about it.'

'Oh,' said Dad. 'Fish fingers, then, is it?'

CHAPTER
4

At dinnertime the next day the telephone rang.

'It's for you,' Mum said, stepping into the lounge. 'A Mr William Peters, wanting to know if you're coming out to play. Shall I tell him to "stuff off" as per yesterday's instructions – or have we had sufficient time to cool off now?'

I sighed and dragged myself off the couch.

'Dinner in fifteen minutes,' said Mum. 'Scrambled eggs. Not negotiable.'

I grunted in acknowledgement and picked up the phone. 'Yeah? Whaddya want?'

'It's me,' he said.

'So?'

'You know.'

'What?' I said.

'You coming out, like?'

I paused to let him stew. 'Dunno. Maybe.'

He seemed to take this as a positive sign. 'Ewan's here. He's got a new ball. We're going to the park. You still got a bag on?'

'No,' I lied.

'You coming, then?'

'*Dunno.* I haven't had my dinner yet.'

He gave a disappointed sigh. 'We're still mates, aren't we?'

'*Course* we were. I'd always been total best mates with Billy.

'It's only a poxy video,' he said.

I ground my teeth and he quickly changed the subject. 'Ewan saw Marcia on the park, coming over.'

Marcia? What was *she* doing here? She lived in Cottersthorpe, miles away.

'She was with Ffion Griffiths,' Billy went on. 'Just walking, Ewan says. They picked a flower and sat on a bench.'

'Thrilling,' I said.

But he knew I was jamming. 'It'll be your bad luck if Marcia turns up and you're stuck at home having your din-dins, won't it?'

'Get lost. Didn't say I *wouldn't* come, did I?'

'Tidy,' he said. 'So we're mates again?'

'Maybe,' I sniffed. It was what I wanted.

'See you in a bit, then,' Billy rapped happily. 'Footie and Marcia. Brilliant. Phwooaar!'

I arrived at the park about twenty minutes later, after wolfing a plate of scrambled eggs on toast. I'd barely jumped off my mountain bike when Scott gave a cheer and stroked the ball towards me. 'Newton – sees Miller in space,' he gabbled.

'Miller looks up,' I continued breathily, sprinting into the path of the ball. 'He spots a stick of rhubarb floating unmarked at the far post. He chips in a dangerous-looking cross and . . .'

'Peters!' screamed Billy, lunging at it. He timed his dive to perfection and met the ball squarely in the centre of his forehead. Ewan, in goal, could only watch it whizz past.

Scott and I both whooped with delight and quickly piled in on top of Billy. He lay on his back with his arms outstretched, soaking up all the adoration he could get. Part of me wanted to smash his face in for being such a prat on the way home yesterday. But I couldn't help being impressed with his style. He was really on top of his form right now. I'd never seen him play with such confidence. If he kept his diving to headers like that, I'd never need to worry about his video again.

'An astonishing goal by Peters,' he chirruped. 'Left the keeper completely—'

I unburied my head from Billy's armpit to see what had made him catch his breath. Marcia and Ffion were thirty metres away. They were cutting across the corner of the park, heading for the path that wound past the swings.

'Wow,' breathed Scott.

My thoughts precisely.

She was wearing jeans and a short black coat, her hands stuffed deep into its fur-trimmed pockets. She looked really classy out of uniform; at least another year older again. As she came nearer she laughed at something and looped her hair back behind one ear.

'Wow, she's had her hair done,' Scott said drippily. His eyes went as wide as a week-old puppy.

We all studied Marcia's hair. The straight blonde lines had been clipped to a bob, ends curling neatly under her chin. I remembered, then, that Ffion's mum did hairdressing at home. So that's what Marcia was doing down here: having her hair re-styled.

'Awesome,' gasped Billy, still on the ground. Even upside-down and flat on his back, Marcia was irresistible, it seemed.

Sadly (for Billy) it wasn't mutual. Suddenly aware they were being observed, Ffion nudged

Marcia and pointed us out. Marcia gave an indifferent shrug. Ffion pulled a stupid, leery face. Billy rolled over and pulled one back.

Then it was war.

Ffion spotted our ball and scooped it up. 'Marcie!' she cried, starting an impromptu netball session.

'Oi!' went Ewan. He took a pace forward, thought better of it and turned to the rest of us. 'Well, someone go and get it off them!'

I stumbled forward and heard Ffion warn: 'Look out, Marcie, one of them's coming.'

Marcia turned to face me, hands around the ball. She licked a loose strand of her hair from her mouth, rocked on her heels and teed up a basket – a waste-paper basket at the side of the path. Covering its bottom was a split bag of chips, smothered in stale tomato sauce.

'Danny, stop her!' the others shouted.

Plop. Too late. Ball in sauce.

Now we knew why she played goal shooter.

I tried really hard to look unimpressed. I folded my arms and cocked my head and let this smirk play over my face. Mum calls it my 'dark and moody' look. Whenever I do it she laughs and says, 'Ooh, that'll drive the girls wild one day'. I wouldn't say Marcia went *wild* exactly, but as she backed away I thought she held my gaze about half a second longer than she needed to. Long enough to look me up and down, anyway.

With a deep sigh Ewan rescued the ball and cleaned it doggedly on the grass. 'Can we play some serious footie now, please?'

'In a minute,' said Billy. 'Watch this first. Marcia, come and get it!' he grunted, gyrating his hips like a bent wheel on a broken bike.

'Yeah, right,' said Scott. 'Like *you* would really have a chance with Marcia.'

To prove Scott right, Marcia turned round and showed Billy a finger.

'Huh, doesn't know what she's missing,' he sniffed.

'Rhubarb, rhubarb, rhubarb,' mocked Scott.

'You were eyeing her too,' sneered Billy. ' "Ooh, she's had her hair done," ' he said, all girly. And even I had to snicker at that, especially as Scott had turned redder than a cherry.

He folded his arms and scowled at us. 'Just 'cos you can't afford the goods doesn't mean to say you can't go shopping.'

'Eh?' went Billy and me together.

Ewan rolled his eyes and bounced the ball hard. 'I think he means she's out of our league. Anyway, she goes with older lads. They all do. That's what Craig, my stepbrother, says: it's something to do with their genes, he reckons.'

We all thought about that a moment.

'Marcia looks cool in jeans,' said Billy.

Ewan smacked a hand against his forehead. 'Not jeans jeans, stupid. *Genes*. Ah look, who cares about flipping girls? Are we having a game of footie or what?'

'Game,' we said and all knocked fists.

Billy suggested two on two.

'How can we if Ewan's in goal?' said Scott.

Ewan lobbed the ball to me. 'What if Danny and Billy attack, but only Billy can score?'

A glint appeared in the rhubarb's eye. 'Yeah,' he said. 'Good idea.'

I should have known all along what was in his mind. We'd only been playing a couple of minutes when I threaded a neat pass through Scott's legs and Billy turned quickly and swept towards goal. He was ten yards out, looking certain to score, when Scott recovered and made his challenge.

'Aww!' Billy yelped and fell flat on his face. He rolled over and over, clutching his ankle. The ball bobbled safely away from goal. I looked at Ewan. We both looked at Scott.

'What?' he said, showing us his palms.

'You didn't have to do that,' Ewan muttered.

'Do what?' said Scott. 'I never touched him.'

Ewan glanced my way, wanting a decision. The law of the park was simple enough: any players

35

not directly involved in a dispute had to vote fairly on what action they thought a referee would take. Ewan passed judgement. 'Penalty,' he said.

'No way!' yelled Scott.

My heart began to thump. Had Billy dived or had Scott chopped him? I looked at Billy. He had his sock rolled down, examining his ankle. Surely he wouldn't cheat on a mate? I pointed to the spot.

Billy immediately leaped to his feet.

'See!' Scott shouted. 'He's not even limping.'

'It's just a game,' said Ewan, taking up position.

'Yeah, well you can *stuff* it,' said Scott. And he stormed off before we could reason with him.

Billy didn't seem to care or notice. He set the ball down twelve yards from goal and gleefully slotted the penalty home, sending Ewan the wrong way entirely.

In truth, he had sent us all the wrong way.

And that was just the beginning.

CHAPTER 5

In the third round of the Inter-Schools Cup we got the worst possible draw imaginable: Cuff Lane Grammar, a school we'd never beaten. We thought we were sunk, and for the first ten minutes we played like it. Only a series of squandered opportunities prevented the Cuffs from taking the lead.

While we were soaking up the early pressure, Billy wasn't seeing too much of the ball – until Scott knocked a clearance out to the wing, Hywel Dennis chipped it hopefully forward and Billy, coming deep, trapped it calmly underfoot. He dragged the ball sideways, gaining space, then set off on a jinking run towards the box. There was a modest splattering of touchline applause. I nearly joined in myself. It was the coolest thing I'd ever seen him do.

But the best was still to come.

As we all charged forward to give him support, Billy homed in on the biggest defender and made like he was going to ghost straight through him. The Cuff Lane gorilla had other ideas. No stick-insect striker was going by *him*. But as the tackle came in, Billy seemed to sprout wings. His arms went up and he tumbled through the air like he'd bounced off the front of a speeding truck.

The gorilla gawped in confusion. He looked down at his hairy, outstretched thigh. There should have been a player spread-eagled across it. But the player was lying face down in the mud.

Pheep!

The referee flapped a bright-yellow card. 'You can cut that out, number three,' he growled. 'One more shocker like that and you're off.'

'Never touched him, ref,' the gorilla grunted, innocently trowelling the air with his hands.

'Direct free kick,' the referee said, dropping the ball outside the area. He waved the Cuff Lane defenders back. They were still muttering on about rubbish decisions when Ryan Jones touched the ball sideways to me and I curled in a shot that their awestruck goalie could only wave at.

It was the first of my four 'illegal' goals: two free kicks, two more from the penalty spot. All of them 'won' by Billy (Quack) Peters. When the final whistle went, people clapped me on the back, shook me by the hand and tousled my hair. 'Got a real future, that lad,' they said. 'Sweetest right foot I've seen since Beckham. Six–one. Their name's on the Cup this year, all right.'

But for certain people our name was dirt. There were boos and hisses from the Cuff Lane supporters as the first of our players left the field. Suddenly a nasty scuffle developed and Mr Crozier had to put himself between Billy and the dad of one of the Cuff Lane boys.

'Tell me something,' the man said, flaring. 'Has that lad got a knife and fork up his shirt?'

'What are you on about?' Mr Crozier stormed.

'I'm on about the fact that your number nine made a meal of every challenge my lad put near him! And you're no better!' he roared in my face, prodding me with an ugly finger. 'I suppose you think you're clever, don't you? Profiting from your best mate's pantomime tricks!'

'Ignore it,' Mr Crozier instructed, pushing me towards the changing rooms.

Scott joined in with an arm around my shoulder. 'Come on,' he said, tugging me away. Then a glob of dirt hit Scott on the back and he turned and yelled, '*Who wants to start?*' Mr Crozier had to lift him off the ground to restrain him. The ref flashed Scott a yellow card. And then Mr Crozier was bellowing at the *ref*. I just couldn't believe that any of this was happening.

I walked on alone, kicking divots into space, gathering my shirt up into my fist. This was all Billy's fault. Billy and his stupid *Strike Hard* video. I felt like tearing his head right off.

Just inside the changing rooms, I got my chance.

As I walked through the doors he jumped on my shoulders and demanded I give him a piggy-back ride. He was whooping and hollering about Willowbrook being the best and saying we were going to win the Cup for sure.

'Get off,' I said, just irritable at first.

It was when he poured the water on my head that I flipped. I backed up with him, right to the wall. There was a bony thud as his back collided with the cold, damp tiles; a yelp when he scraped his ear on a coat hook. He came at me then in a flurry of fists. Soon we were gripping each other's hair and wrestling our way to the changing-room floor. That was where Mr Crozier found us.

'All right, what's this?!' He hoiked us up and pulled us apart, holding us both at the end of an arm.

Billy cried out: 'He started it, sir!'

'You started it!' I railed, trying to throw myself forward. Mr Crozier held me back. I scowled into Billy's mud-stained face. He knew what I meant: the *Strike Hard* video. But neither of us was going to admit it.

Mr Crozier tightened his grip on our shirts. 'I don't care which of you started it,' he growled. 'It's bad enough scrapping with the opposition, never mind kicking chunks out of your own blessed team. Fighting is a serious disciplinary offence. Be grateful I don't give you both a two-match suspension. And the same goes for you,' he bawled at Scott. '*You* should be thankful you only got a booking. If I hadn't intervened when I did, you might be on the wrong end of a referee's report.'

'Yes, sir,' said Scott, wringing his hands.

Mr Crozier glared at Billy. 'I want to see you in my office on Monday.'

'Why?' asked Hywel. 'What's he done?'

'That's *my* business,' Mr Crozier snapped. 'Right, I want everyone showered and out of this room in *twenty* minutes. Triple press-ups for any boy who's late.'

That caused a frantic scrabble of studs. My fight with Billy was completely forgotten – by everyone except our captain, Scott. 'What happened?' he whispered, pulling off his shirt. 'Was it that loony that got you going . . . or is it 'cos Billy won't stop diving?'

And that was the moment my injury happened. Whether it was the shock of hearing the truth or the movement as I kicked off my boots I couldn't tell, but the pain was fierce and shockingly intense. A lightning jab in the right of my groin. I pressed my hands against the front of my shorts and almost propelled my head against the wall.

'What's the matter?' gasped Scott, looking alarmed. 'Danny, what's the matter? Sir? *Sir?!*'

'Shut up-pp!' I hissed. 'It's just a pull. Don't get Crozzy. You know what he's like.' Mr Crozier took a very strict line with injuries: health first, team second. The slightest doubt about any boy's fitness was enough to make him rewrite the team sheet, no matter how vital the player was.

Scott tugged my sleeve. 'Can you get to the showers?'

I nodded. The pain had eased already. It was little more than a dull throb now.

'Come on,' he said, 'let's get in quick. It'll do you in if you have to do press-ups.'

'Hurry up, you pair!' Mr Crozier barked.

'Yessir,' said Scott, shielding me from him. 'You've gotta rest it,' he hissed. 'All weekend. Or you won't be fit for training on Tuesday.'

'Shut up,' I said. 'I'll be all right.'

Scott wasn't convinced. 'I'll call round on Sunday, about two o'clock. Just to make sure you're feeling OK.'

'You're worse than my flipping mum,' I tutted.

'I'm the captain,' he sniffed. 'It's my job.'

CHAPTER 6

I rested, just as Scott had suggested. I spent all Friday night reading *Kick!* magazine, flat on my back, eating peanuts and crisps. On Saturday I drew some graphs for maths, then played a tournament of *Soccer Millennium* on my computer. I was stuck away in my room so long that when I came down to watch the football that evening Mum pretended not to know me. 'I'm sorry,' she said. 'You can't sit there. My son has been abducted by an alien species. We keep his place ready in the faint hope that he might be returned to our midst some day.'

'Yes, Mum,' I sighed, and flopped onto the sofa.

'Cheer up,' she said, 'it might never happen.'
She ruffled my hair and headed for the door.

'Problem?' asked Dad in a disembodied voice.
He was sitting in his chair, eyes glued to the telly.

'No,' I said quietly. But it wasn't the truth. By
now I'd worked out what had really made me
blow when Billy had wanted his piggy-back ride.
It was all to do with what that bloke had said about
'profiting from my best mate's pantomime tricks'.
I'd tried to ignore it, like Crozzy had said, but it
hurt – 'cos I knew it was partly true. The thing that
was chewing me up was this: I could prove that
Billy Peters was diving, but I wasn't doing anything at all to stop it. In fact, I was probably making
it worse. Every time the duck won a free kick or
penalty, I was the one who had to make something
of it; I had to turn those chances into goals. In a
way, I was every bit as guilty of cheating as he was.

'No way,' Dad muttered, breaking into my
thoughts.

I looked up and saw him frowning at the screen.
They were showing a dubious penalty decision.
Dad kneeled on the floor and tilted his head, trying
to get a better angle on the replay.

'Ridiculous,' he muttered, as the striker went
down. 'The defender pulled his leg away, surely?
I don't think he even made contact, do you?'

On the telly, the studio experts agreed. 'Blatant

dive,' said the dark-haired one with the thick Scottish accent. He tightened his lips and shuffled in his chair. 'If I was the referee an' I saw that, that striker would be walkin' – no question about it. Shockin'. Drags the game right into the gutter. Best of it is, he gets up and takes the penalty kick! Unbelievable. How can he do it?'

'Because he's paid to,' said Dad. 'They should get me on this programme. I'd put them right.'

So I decided to test him out. 'Dad, you think diving's cheating, don't you?'

'Um,' he grunted. 'It ought to be stopped.'

'OK, if you were the penalty-taker in a team and your side won a penalty 'cos someone had dived – what would you do?'

'Blast it straight at the goalie,' he declared.

'So he could easily save it, you mean?' Miss? Deliberately? As a sort of protest? I wasn't sure I'd be able to do it.

But it wasn't quite what Dad had meant. ''Course not,' he laughed. 'Why would I want the goalie to save it? If you aimed your shot at the centre of the goal, chances are the keeper would shift to one side – and bingo, you're a goal to the good.'

'You'd still try to score, you mean?'

Dad gave me a puzzled look. 'That's the usual idea with a penalty, isn't it?'

I picked at a fraying patch on my jeans. Somehow, I thought, he'd missed the point.

On Sunday morning I just couldn't settle. For three and a half hours I moped around the house, not knowing what to do with myself. Mum told me off twice for getting under her feet (she threatened to hoover me if I didn't get off the couch); and even when I went upstairs to my room, Dad warned me if I didn't turn my stereo down he'd come up and glue some headphones to my ears. 'Why don't you go to the park?' they kept saying. 'It's glorious weather. Give Billy a ring.' Huh. That was easy for them to say. They hadn't been tugging his hair out in the changing rooms. They hadn't been telling him what a cheat he was. Anyway, football was off the agenda: I had a pulled muscle to rest.

About half-past twelve I was locked in the loo, feeling my groin to see if it hurt, when I heard Mum and Dad in the bathroom next door. They were having one of their 'serious' discussions.

'What's got into him?' Mum was saying.

'Hormones,' said Dad. 'That's my guess.'

'Oh, heck,' Mum sighed. 'Perhaps Alice was right. I was hoping we'd escape that for another year at least.'

Escape? Escape what? It was like they were talking about a guinea pig or something.

47

Dad said, 'Hold this spanner, will you?'

There was a clanking of pipes. Mum went on: 'You think he's moping about this girl?'

Girl? What *girl*?

'Alice says he's locking himself in the loo half a dozen times a day.'

Dad cleared his throat. 'Well. You know. It's normal . . . at his age.'

Huh?

'Well, what do you suggest?' asked Mum.

'Caution,' said Dad. 'The softly, softly approach. 'I—' *Clank!* 'Oh, flipping heck! Get me a cloth! I think this valve is going to blow!'

End of serious conversation.

At dinnertime everything came to a head. As we all sat down at the dining-room table, Mum rubbed a knuckle down my cheek and said: 'Come on, Danny. We've all been through it.'

Pardon? Through *what*?

Then Alice piped up. 'Guess what, everyone?'

Dad buttered a slice of bread and said, 'Someone's won you in a competition and they're coming to collect you later tonight?'

Alice swung her ponytail and pointed at me. 'He used *two* lots of shampoo on his hair this morning.'

Mum frowned and passed the gravy to Dad. 'What's your point, Alice?'

'He wants to look nice for *Marcia*,' she toadied.

So I flicked a forkful of mashed potato at her. It wasn't exactly the cleverest of moves. Alice yelped and kicked the leg of Dad's chair, causing Dad to let go of the gravy jug. The gravy splattered into his lap. As he jumped up, swearing, grabbing his trousers, trying not to let the gravy seep through, he stood on Millie's tail and made her yowl. She hissed and lashed out at the first thing human.

'Agh!' cried Mum and banged the table. Two glasses of milk, one half-pint of lager, one orange squash and a small dish of mint sauce all tipped up.

Dad's trousers, the tablecloth, Alice's blouse and jumper and one of Mum's socks had to go into the washing machine.

I was sent to my room in disgrace.

While I was there, the doorbell rang. I looked at my watch. Two o'clock. Scott. I hurried to the top of the stairs.

'I'm sorry, Scott,' Dad was saying. 'Danny's been rather silly today.'

'Oh,' said Scott, looking Dad up and down. Dad was the one who looked rather silly. He still hadn't got any trousers on.

'He's grounded,' said Dad. 'You'll have to see him at school tomorrow.'

I sighed and grabbed the banister rail.

'Is he all right?' Scott asked worriedly. 'He's not . . . *hurt*, is he?'

I thought I heard Dad grind his teeth. 'He'll have a few sore muscles by the time I've finished with him.'

'Sore muscles?!' gasped Scott.

'He's going to get a job – or three,' said Dad.

'I want to help him!' Scott said immediately.

I don't think Dad could quite believe that. He drummed his fingers on the door frame a second, then yelled out: 'Danny! Come down!'

I was there in seconds. Dad flashed us both a distrustful look. 'It appears that Scott would like to share your punishment.'

'Oh,' I said.

Scott just grinned.

Dad said, 'Do you know what a lawn is, Scott?'

'Yes, Mr Miller.'

'Good, in the shed you'll find a machine for cutting it.'

'Right you are,' said Scott. He beamed like a lighthouse. 'I'll park my bike round the back then, shall I?'

CHAPTER 7

Scott asked me a zillion times how I was. A zillion times I replied, 'OK.' I hadn't had a single tweak from my groin since that jab in the changing rooms on Friday afternoon. But Scott wasn't taking any chances. 'I'll do all the hard stuff,' he said. 'You just try to look . . . busy.'

So while he mowed, I raked up the cuttings. He clipped the hedge; I brushed up the bits. We talked about football practically non-stop. But neither of us mentioned Billy Peters until, that is, we were cleaning the car.

'Why do you think Crozzy wants to see him?' Scott asked, busily hoovering the driver's seat.

I dunked a sponge in a bucket of water and shrugged.

'I reckon it's about him diving, don't you?'

'Maybe,' I said, feeling tight inside. I slapped the sponge down with a squelch on the bonnet.

'Why do you think he's started doing it?'

''Cos he's useless,' I said, 'and he thinks he looks big. Him and his stupid *Strike Hard* video.' I gritted my teeth and rubbed at a bird dropping, wishing it was Billy's grinning face.

'Video?' said Scott, retreating, bum-first, out of the car.

I squeezed a soapy waterfall onto the drive. I'd been so absorbed in my personal mutterings I hadn't heard the drone of the hoover stop.

'Did you say he'd got a video? About playing striker?'

It was hopeless. He'd got me totally trapped. I had no choice but to tell him what I knew.

His expression turned from curious to furious in a second. 'That's why he dived on the park,' he muttered. 'He was practising – on me. Creep. I'm gonna *do* him. I got booked because of him. It was his fault all that trouble started after we stuffed Cuff Lane on Friday.'

'Well at least no-one called you a cheat,' I said, splatting the sponge down into the bucket. Now that Billy's secret was out, I was determined I was going to have my say. I told Scott what was on my mind – all the guilt I was feeling about Billy diving.

'But that's different,' he argued, zapping a dead leaf into the hoover. 'It's bad if a mate starts cheating on a mate, but in a match it's sort of . . . OK, I s'pose. Loads of Premier League players do it.'

'So? That doesn't make it right.'

'I know, but I read in the papers once that if the England players got a knock in the box they're s'posed to go down and appeal for a penalty.'

'Scott, we're not England, and Billy's not playing the *game* any more. He's just showing off, waiting for the chance for someone to crop him. Then he's expecting me to score.'

'Well, shall I take the penalties from now on, then?'

'No! That's not the *point*. It doesn't matter who takes the penalties, does it? If *you'd* scored four, it'd be just as bad.'

'Fat chance,' he scoffed, but he could see I was serious and changed his tone accordingly. 'What do you wanna do about it, then?'

Stop Billy diving. That was obvious. The problem was how.

Scott took a second to think. 'OK, I've got a plan. I'll sneak round to Billy's house tonight, grab the video and stick it accidentally-on-purpose in his mum's microwave.'

'Brilliant,' I tutted. 'Except he probably knows it off by heart, by now.'

'OK. How about . . . erasing his memory with a magnet? I saw that once in a film on the telly.'

'*Scott.*' I gave him a look.

'What then?' he said, sounding slightly fed up. 'You think of something.'

I looked away, pained. I did have an idea. I was just building up the nerve to suggest it. 'What if the whole team got together and you told Billy he's got to pack it in?'

'You're joking,' he spluttered. 'He'll think I'm nuts. And Hywel and Ryan'll never agree. They think the duck's dead brilliant. They're really big mates with him now.'

Somewhere deep inside, that hurt.

'Anyway,' Scott went on, 'Crozzy's gonna roast him on Monday, isn't he? He's the manager. He's gotta sort it.'

Just then, the kitchen door swished open and Dad stepped out with a plate of sandwiches. He had a newspaper tucked underneath one arm. He looked the car over and frowned. 'Taking your time with this job, aren't you? You've still got to clean out the rabbit, remember?'

Scott looked at Bigfoot's cage and sighed.

Dad rested the plate on the roof of the car. 'Your soft-hearted mother thinks you should eat.'

'Thanks,' said Scott, snapping up something tomatoey with cheese.

Dad landed the paper across my chest. 'Here. Thought you might find this article of interest as you were quizzing me about it yesterday.'

'What is it?' said Scott, dribbling tomato.

Dad nodded at the paper. 'They're starting a campaign to stamp out diving, all the way down to schoolboy level.'

I checked the headline. My heart missed a beat.

DIVING ME MAD

THE POISON RUINING OUR NATIONAL GAME

by Bryan Pringle, football correspondent

'It's about that penalty last night,' said Scott, grabbing the paper and poring over it. 'Did you see? It was never a foul.'

He meant the incident I'd watched with Dad. Apart from the usual squabbles on the pitch, there had also been trouble in the players' tunnel afterwards. Several players had been booked for fighting. One of the home team's coaching staff had been hit by a missile thrown from the crowd. It sounded just like the Cuff Lane incident. A 'flashpoint', Bryan Pringle had called it.

'Listen to this bit,' Scott blabbed on as Dad flapped a hand and left us to it. 'It says players who dive are a disgrace to the game. "Their boggus—"'

'Bogus,' I corrected.

'"Their bogus histrionics are having a disruptive influence on our younger generation." Do you think that means us?'

'Dunno. Let me see.'

'I'll read it,' he insisted, leaning further away. '"Only last week I was appalled to see my eight-year-old nephew rolling away from a phantom tackle like tumbleweed blowing through the ghost of football past." What's tumbleweed?'

'Give it here,' I tutted, trying to snatch the paper off him. Again he shrugged it off. He mumbled his way through a few more sentences, then finally read out something of interest:

'"That is why 'Pringle on Sunday' is backing a motion to penalize teams with persistent offenders."'

'What?' I said, concealing a shiver.

Scott speared the paper with the tip of his finger. '"There is a steadily growing voice of opinion which believes that clubs who field players consistently cautioned for simulating fouls should have league points deducted *or* be disqualified from cup competitions – with immediate effect."'

Tuk-tuk, went Bigfoot and hopped into his hide.

'Just if someone *dives*?' I said.

Scott nodded and passed me the paper. And there it was, in black and white.

'Flipping heck, listen to *this*,' I said. ' "Referees, supporters, managers, scouts – all have a duty to weed out the cheats, right the way down from the international arena to our local parks and schoolboy pitches." '

We exchanged a worried glance.

'You'd better be right about Crozzy,' I said.

CHAPTER

8

I took my time getting ready for school the next morning, knowing that if we caught the later bus there was far less chance of bumping into Billy. I couldn't face any awkward confrontations with him, not after what Scott and I had discovered yesterday.

The delay, however, did not suit Alice. My sister is one of those barmy kids who really love school and hate to miss a minute. At half-past eight she tracked me down. I was in the loo, feeling around my groin, when she rattled the handle and yelled downstairs, 'Mu-um! Danny's locked himself in the toilet *again*!'

'Danny!' Mum barked from the foot of the stairs. 'What are you doing?'

A fitness test. (What did she *think* I was doing?)

'Get a move on!' she warned. 'You'll be late for school.'

I zipped up my trousers and flushed the loo.

As it happened, we did miss the early bus. Alice whinged all the way to school. 'You're dead,' she kept muttering. 'Deader than dog poo. Deader than the deadest deaded-out dead thing.'

'Shut up,' I said, sliding down in my seat. The last thing I needed was Alice giving me a load of grief.

But as we stepped off the bus at Willowbrook Avenue, Alice was soon to be the least of my problems. She was scooting on ahead towards the primary school, shouting that she hated me worse than cold porridge, when a car pulled up and a girl got out. It was Jenifer Williams. Marcia's sister.

Alice's friend.

'Hiya,' they hailed one another. Jeni reached down and pulled up a sock. Normally, they would have gone haring up the road. But that morning, Alice flagged Jeni to a halt. She cupped her hands around Jeni's ear, whispered something and pointed at me. Jeni giggled like mad – and pointed at the car. The door was still ajar.

Right on cue, two buckle-shoed, white-socked legs appeared. They flexed at the knee and the toes of the shoes dibbled blindly for the pavement. They were followed by four centimetres of pale-pink thigh, then a hand clutching the hem of a skirt, then . . .

Whumph! A group of tag-playing juniors shot past. One of them barged me so hard in the back that I stumbled forward and my workbook shot out from under my arm. All my graphs for Mr Dunlop's class flapped through the air like autumn leaves. Alice and Jeni exploded with laughter. I got five of the graphs in as many seconds. The last was under Marcia's foot.

My eyes travelled slowly from her shoes to her face.

'You again,' she said, looping her hair.

Me. Yes. Mr Wobbly Knees. I didn't know what to say.

Jenifer Williams filled in for me: 'He loves you, Marcie!'

Alice snorted like a pig and clenched her fists. I prayed for a burst of sister-dissolving acid rain. To my amazement, my wish was almost granted:

'Yeah, 'course he does,' Marcia said tiredly. 'Now run away to school and play, *little girls.*'

Alice's smug grin switched to a look of absolute betrayal. She scowled at Jeni. Jeni scowled back. They wiggled their tongues at Marcia's back. Marcia didn't give them a second look. She bent down primly and rescued the graph. 'It was going to go under the car,' she said, brushing off the dirt and handing it over. 'My footprint's messed up your pie chart – sorry. Bet Dunlop'll make you do it again.'

''S'all right,' I mumbled, with a little shrug. A tiddly little pie chart wouldn't take long. Besides, I could always *frame* the original: 10p for a glimpse of Marcia's footprint; I could probably make a fortune, showing it round the yard.

'So,' she said, with a gentle accent, 'you're Daniel Miller, then?'

'Yes,' I replied, a bit red-faced.

She casually examined the state of her nails. 'Saw you on Willowbrook Park last week. Thought you were gonna chase me, I did.' Her green eyes flickered across my face.

'I only wanted the ball back,' I said.

Marcia smiled thinly and changed the subject. 'It's funny I should bump into you again; you play football for the middle school, don't you?'

'Yes,' I said.

We started to walk.

'What number do you wear?'

'Pardon?' I said.

'What number?' she tutted. 'On your *shirt*?'

'Ten,' I answered, having to think. Why would Marcia want to know that?

She tapped her immaculate fingertips together, then slowly unclipped her bag. From it she pulled a small red notebook. She turned a few pages, then read out: ' "W10: Gifted midfielder. Two good feet. Passing and distribution first rate. Extremely dangerous in <u>dead-ball situations</u>" – whatever that means. "Nucleus of team. County level." ' She snapped the book shut. 'You're quite good at football, aren't you?'

I stared at her, open-mouthed. 'Where'd you get that book?'

She fanned it teasingly under her chin. 'We had a netball match on Saturday morning. I found it on the drive, just under a car. I was going to hand it in to Mr Crozier, but . . .'

'I'll give it to Crozzy for you!' I stuck out my hand and immediately dropped my workbook again. This time she didn't bother to help me.

'Hmm, don't know about that,' she simpered, swinging round and walking away. 'It sounds quite valuable to me, this book. Shall I read you some more?'

I gathered up the graphs and scrambled after her.

' "W5. Strong in tackle. Reads game well, but

suspect on crosses. Danger going forwards."
Who's that?'

'Scott Newton,' I replied.

'Is he that horrible skinny twerp?'

I shook my head. 'That's Billy Peters.'

'What number's he?'

I told her. She looked up W9. 'Hmm. He's "cunning", according to this.'

'Show me,' I begged.

She held it hidden, flat to her chest. 'If I was one of your mates,' she said, 'you'd offer to do me a swap for it, wouldn't you?'

I shrugged and said, 'S'pose. What do you want?'

'Not sure,' she said with a click of her tongue. 'I'll think about it.'

But I didn't have time for that. 'Marcia,' I gulped, 'can I . . . *borrow* the book, please – while you're thinking about it?'

'Pff!' she went. 'You're a cheeky one.'

I lowered my head.

'But you're sort of . . . *cute* with it.'

Bang! Something thudded inside my jacket. I knew it could only be one of three things: my pocket calculator had just exploded, Bigfoot had sneaked inside my shirt, or my heart was thumping like a bongo drum.

Bongo! Bongo! Bongo!

It had to be my heart.

'OK, it's a deal,' she chirped. She held out the book.

I fished for it.

She immediately pulled it back. 'You definitely promise to do me a swap?'

'Honest,' I said as we turned through the gates.

'I'll tell Mr Crozier if you try to sneak out of it.'

'Promise,' I said.

'With knobs on?'

'Double.'

She hit me again with those big green eyes. 'What if said I wanted a—?'

Drrinnngggg! The first bell went.

We slowed to a halt. My heart was pounding. Wanted a . . . what? She stepped forward and picked some fluff off my jacket. 'Typical; saved by the bell.' She pushed the notebook into my hand. 'I'll be in touch,' she said, in a voice like softly lapping water. She wiggled her fingers and turned away.

Suddenly, Scott materialized beside me, his eyes as big as milk-bottle tops. We watched Marcia merge in with a group of other girls and disappear into the science block. 'You . . . she . . . *how*?' he gasped.

'Dunno. She just stopped and talked to me. She called me cute. She gave me something.'

'A lovebite?' he said, inspecting my neck.

'Don't be dumb – it's better than that.'

'Get a move on, you boys!' a teacher shouted.

Scott and I broke into a trot. 'Go slower,' he advised. 'You're resting, remember. There's a meeting at break, in the gym, with Crozzy. I think it's about the quarter-final. What's that book?'

'Marcia found it by the pitch. Someone's been making notes about us.'

'Who?'

I flipped the book open, right at my page: 'Nucleus of team. County level.' 'A scout, I think.'

'Wow,' gasped Scott, and we hurried into school.

CHAPTER 9

There was no time to study the book before break. Scott pestered me like mad throughout human geography, but I couldn't risk the book being confiscated. Mr Featherby, our teacher, is strict on 'tomfoolery'. He split me and Billy up ages ago for scribbling the names of football stadiums on a fold-out map of European nations. At the time, we had both been really miffed. But that morning I was glad we were six desks apart. All I had in common with the duck right now was 'the growth of populations in the third world' for an hour and a bit – and that was how it was going to stay.

When the bell went, I charged for the door

only to hear Mr Featherby boom: 'I want a volunteer to take a globe to the library. Daniel Miller, you'll do.'

'Sir, I don't want to volunteer,' I protested. 'There's a football meeting in the gym at break.'

'Well, a sprint up the stairs should keep you fit. It might also sharpen your wits. I assume from that desperately puzzled frown that you thought I hadn't heard your "joke" last week about Ben Nevis being "that bloke" who plays in goal for Partick Thistle?'

Scott offered me a sympathetic look.

'The globe on the cupboard,' Mr Featherby said. 'It's valuable, Daniel. Please don't drop it.'

I took the stairs to the library two steps at a time. It was only when I swerved to avoid Mr Flint as he lumped a projector screen round a corner that I remembered I ought to be taking it easy. But I hadn't felt a tweak from my groin all morning. That had to be mega-good news. I got a very strange look from Miss Rees, the librarian, as I stuck my hand down my pants to make sure. But she just shook her head and said rather frostily, 'Don't you have somewhere to be, young man?'

The gym. That's where I needed to be. I popped the globe down by an old PC and hurried away for the team meeting.

On the way there, I checked the notebook. The first three entries were for Cuff Lane players. I passed straight over them and went to the pages with a W in the corner. I breezed through a piece about Hywel Dennis; it said he was 'keen, but wild and aggressive'. Ewan Thomas got a tick for 'a safe pair of hands', but a wiggly underline for 'weak kicking out'. Then I found my entry again. It was just as Marcia had read it – with only one bit missing. Towards the foot of the page, circled in red, was the word 'Man'.

'Man'? 'Man' what? Man United? Me?

'Oh, look where you're going,' a cross voice said. Mrs Faversham, our music teacher, made a loud sighing noise and stepped sideways to avoid a head-on collision.

'Sorry, miss,' I muttered.

'I should think so,' she said, and swept into the staff room, muttering to herself.

I hurried on and turned down the long gym corridor – and quickly flicked over the page. W9. Billy Peters.

He had five neat lines of confident writing: 'Tall, ungainly striker. Useful in air. Weaker on ground, but cunning with it. Deceptive, esp. with back to goal. Diver? <u>Watch v. carefully</u>.'

I almost fell into a box of bean bags. Hadn't

Bryan Pringle's article said . . . ? I fished it out and skimmed the last paragraph: 'Referees, supporters, managers, scouts all have a duty to weed out the cheats.' If a scout reported Billy to the Inter-Schools Committee we could be . . .

Just then, Mr Crozier's voice rang out. 'Don't give me that. You know full well what I'm on about, Peters.' I crept up to the office door, in time to see Crozzy reach into a drawer and take out a slim brown envelope. 'That parent I was forced to protect you from on Friday is kicking up a right old stink.'

'Sir?' said Billy, just out of my sight.

Mr Crozier let out an irritated sigh. 'The gentleman who accused you of having a "knife and fork" up your shirt has written a letter of complaint to the school. He is saying – in slightly less colourful terms – that you were "putting yourself about in an ungentlemanly manner". Diving, for want of a better description. This morning I was summoned to Mr Duberry's office to explain what this –' he flapped the letter against Billy's chest – 'was all about. I don't like being hauled into the head's office, Peters. That's your territory. So, come on – what have you got to say for yourself?'

And that was Billy's golden chance. To stop the

trouble before it began. He didn't need to come clean about the *Strike Hard* video. All he had to do was admit he'd been diving and promise it wouldn't happen again.

But he chose to play dirty instead. 'Nothing,' he said.

'*Nothing?!*' barked Crozzy.

'Haven't been diving, sir . . .'

What? I fell back against the wall in shock. How could Billy *lie* like that? Everybody knew he'd been up to it, including, it seemed, a county scout.

Mr Crozier somehow kept his cool. 'Do I look like a donkey to you, Peters?'

Cor, that must have been hard to resist. The chance to go *Ee-yore* in Crozzy's face? But all Billy said was, 'Sir?'

Mr Crozier tapped his desk. 'I'm not thick, lad. And I don't recall seeing a ghost on the pitch: which is the only explanation *I* can come up with for the way you won that second free kick.'

Billy went, 'Sir?'

'Don't try my patience,' Mr Crozier growled. 'When you hit the deck late on in the game there was a good strip of daylight between you and the nearest Cuff Lane boy; whatever brought you down, it wasn't him.'

'I lost my balance,' Billy explained. 'He pushed me outside the area, sir. The referee tried to play the advantage, but when I went down he had to bring play back.'

Mr Crozier said, 'Pull the other one, lad.'

But Billy could do far better than that. 'The referee was closer than you,' he said.

I took two paces away from the door, sure that Billy would be mangled to bits for giving out serious lip like that.

But no. Mr Crozier let it go. 'All right,' he said calmly, 'we'll play it your way. I'll give you the benefit of the doubt . . . *this time*. But if a referee gives you your marching orders, you will be suspended from this football team for a very long time. Do I make myself clear?'

Billy muttered the obligatory, 'Sir.'

Mr Crozier ripped the letter in half. 'Luckily for you I've convinced Mr Duberry that this is just a case of very sour grapes. But if we suffer any more of this kind of thing it could be very serious indeed. I don't just mean for you, my lad, I mean for the team and Willowbrook School. If we get branded a load of cheats, you can take it as read that our name will not be in the hat for next season's trophy. Do you get my drift?'

Suddenly, the door whooshed fully open and Mr Crozier swept out before I could hide. 'Why are you skulking out here?' he barked.

'Had to do an errand for Mr Featherby, sir.' I

kept my head as low as I could, desperate not to catch Billy's eye.

'Well, if you've done it, get to the gym.'

'Yes, sir,' I said, happy to go.

But as I burst through the doors I was anything *but* happy. As I reached Scott's side he nudged me and whispered, 'Billy's been to Crozzy.' He nodded towards the doors of the gym. Mr Crozier came in, looking tight-lipped. Billy went to stand by Hywel Dennis. They exchanged a quick word, then quietly slapped palms. Billy looked totally smug. And I understood, then, why he'd lied to Crozzy: Hywel had put him up to it. Hywel had told him what to say.

Suddenly, I felt really sick inside. This team was in serious trouble. Our problems were a long, long way from over.

CHAPTER 10

'Right,' said Mr Crozier, swinging his arms like the blades of a windmill to touch the toes of each foot in turn. 'Do you want the bad news or the bad news first?'

'Isn't there any good news?' Ryan Jones asked.

'No,' said Crozzy to the floor of the gym. 'Unless you count the fact we've been drawn at home on Friday afternoon.'

'Who against?' asked Scott.

'Bushloe High.'

The name echoed round the window bars. 'Bushloe?' 'That posh lot up the Cottersthorpe Road?' 'They wear green blazers, don't they?'

'Soft,' sneered Hywel.

Mr Crozier stood up straight. He stuck out his chin and jogged on the spot. 'Never judge a team by its dress sense, Dennis. Mind you, when the opposition catch sight of your scruffy locks they'd be forgiven for thinking they were up against Ug from the Stone Age eleven. Are combs banned in your house or something?'

Hywel spat on his hand and tried, unsuccessfully, to smooth his hair.

Mr Crozier pressed on. 'Bushloe High has a serious reputation for sporting achievement. In the last two seasons their under-fourteens have had five players selected for county trials. They are also the current holders of this cup.'

I looked at Scott. His shoulders fell. 'You mean we're gonna get stuffed?' he said.

Mr Crozier did a couple of jerking twists. 'We will, if you don't shut up and listen.' He scooped up a basketball and pressed it hard between his palms. 'A little bird tells me that the present Bushloe team is not the force of previous years. They are reputed, however, to have one player who is rather special.'

'What position does he play in?' Ewan asked.

'Sweeper,' Mr Crozier replied.

I glanced quickly at Billy and saw him knocking fists with Hywel. They were practically wetting their pants – chuffed, no doubt, that the Bushloe star was the last defender: easy fodder for a waddling duck.

'Is he a county player?' asked Scott.

'County trials don't begin for two weeks,' said Mr Crozier. 'Even so, I think it's safe to assume that this boy will be up there, pushing for selection.'

'Is he big?' asked Ryan.

'I don't know,' said Mr Crozier. He lobbed the basketball high at the net. It went in sweetly without touching the ring. 'My "mole" wouldn't give me any more details. We are simply to watch out for an "A. Woodruff" who plays deep, across the back. So, in Games this week, I propose to look at ways of dealing with a typical sweeper system.'

'Easy,' I heard Billy hiss to Hywel. Hywel quacked quietly. My stomach rolled.

'Miller, what's the matter?' Mr Crozier asked. He'd seen me tighten and was giving me the eye.

'Nothing, sir,' I said with a shake of my head. But I couldn't stop my hand drifting over my guts. Something strange was happening down there. I glanced at the clock. A minute to the bell. If I could just hold out, I could get to the bogs. If only Mr Crozier hadn't gone and said . . .

'Well, you look like you've swallowed an onion, raw.'

That did it. I started to heave.

'Oh, for crying out loud!' Mr Crozier exclaimed. He marched straight over and forced me into a kneeling position. 'Bucket, someone! Come on, look sharp! I've got a badminton class in here after break. I don't want my shuttlecocks soaked in vomit.'

Scott hurried over to kneel beside me. 'You all right?' he said, adding in a whisper: 'You know, *down there*?'

''Course he's all right,' Mr Crozier barked. 'It's pre-match nerves, that's all.'

Hrrrp! I went.

'Oh, *yuk*,' went Scott.

'WHERE THE HELL IS THAT BUCKET?!' Mr Crozier thundered.

CHAPTER 11

'Sickness?' Mrs Woolbury, the matron, queried. 'Daniel Miller? That's not like you. Sit up here. I'll check your temperature.' She patted a long black couch. I pushed myself onto it, letting my legs dangle over the side. Mrs Woolbury opened a small glass cabinet. She took out a thermometer and flicked it several times. 'How bad was this vomiting?'

'Bad,' said Scott. 'He nearly yakked on Crozzy's trainers.'

Mrs Woolbury closed the cabinet with a terse little click. 'Don't you have a lesson to go to, young man?'

'Only English,' Scott replied – adding quickly as she frowned: 'Mr Crozier said someone should stay with him, miss. We've got to play Bushloe High on Friday. Do you think you can cure him by then?'

'I'll do my best,' she said. She put a hand round my wrist to check my pulse and pushed the thermometer under my tongue.

Just then the telephone rang. 'Won't be a moment,' Mrs Woolbury said, and drifted away to answer it.

As soon as she had turned, Scott pointed to my groin. 'Was it that,' he hissed, 'that made you throw?'

I shook my head and pulled the notebook from my pocket, turning up the page marked W9. 'A schout's sheen Billy, like Bryan Pringle shaid.'

Scott read it through. 'Aw no,' he mumbled. 'He knows Billy dives.'

'Yeah, an' ish gonna get worsh,' I said. I held the thermometer off my tongue and explained what I'd overheard in the corridor and what I'd seen in the gym, with Hywel. 'I bet Billy's told Hywel about the video and everything. He's gonna try it on with Woodruff for sure.'

Scott nodded and bit his lip. 'I say we give this notebook to Crozzy. And that article, too.'

I shook my head. 'It'll look like snitching. Even

Crozzy won't like that. And Hywel'll kill us if he ever finds out.'

Scott grimaced and glanced at the notebook again. 'What does this mean?' He pointed to a bit I hadn't noticed before: the letters ISC, circled near the foot of Billy's entry.

'Don't know,' I said. 'I've got one of those.'

He found my page and read it. 'That must mean Man United,' he gasped. 'Perhaps he's going to send you for a trial at Old Trafford?'

'Well, where's he going to send Billy, then? There isn't a club that begins ISC.'

Scott frowned and muttered the letters aloud. Suddenly, his eyes began to swim with fear. 'What if it stands for Inter-Schools Committee? What if the scout *is* planning to report him, if he sees him diving again?'

Across the room, Mrs Woolbury plonked down the phone. 'Right,' she said, coming to join us. She extracted the thermometer and squinted at the reading. 'Hmm. Temperature's a little higher than ideal, but nothing to worry about.' She slipped her hands round my neck to feel my glands. 'Any headache or dizziness? Pains in the tummy?'

'No! His tummy's great!' barked Scott.

Mrs Woolbury reared like a smoking dragon. 'I wasn't asking you.'

'I'm fine,' I told her. 'Just a bit . . . hungry.'

'Did you have any breakfast this morning?'

'No.'

'Silly boy. Got anything in your bag?'

'Banana, I think.'

She nodded with approval. 'Have it before you go back to class. If anyone complains, you've got my permission.'

'Thanks,' I said and slid off the couch.

'Wait. You'll need a note to show to your teacher, just to explain why you're late for class.' She hastily scribbled something down. 'Give it to your parents when you get home. If you start to feel bad, you come straight back.'

'Yes, miss.' I shoved the note into my pocket, then headed off for English with Scott.

When we walked in, everyone was quiet and writing in their books. Mr Trewent crooked a finger and beckoned us to him. 'And where have you pair been?'

I handed him the note. He ironed it on his desk. 'I see. And what's your excuse, Mr Newton?'

'Had to stay with him, sir. Mr Crozier said.'

Mr Trewent pursed his lips. 'Well, I shall confirm that – or not – with Mr Crozier at lunchtime. Now go and sit down – not you, Daniel.' I stalled and turned to face him. He rocked back in his chair with his fingers steepled. 'For one glorious moment I had hoped this note was a witty demonstration of your homework assignment.'

I blinked, confused.

'Clearly not,' he said. He swung his chair round and clapped his hands. 'Pay attention, please.'

Everyone rested their pens.

'Read it,' he said, nodding at the note. 'Aloud. To the class.' He sat back, tapping his thumbs together.

I read it out, twice. *'Daniel was sent to me . . . mild bout of vomiting.'* It all seemed clear enough. What did Mr Trewent want me to do, shove two fingers down my throat to prove it?

'Well?' he asked.

'I don't understand, sir.'

Mr Trewent scanned the class. 'Someone remind him of his homework this week.'

'Anonymity, sir,' Avril Shaughnessy said.

'Thank you.' Mr Trewent pinned me with his gaze. 'Ring any bells?'

No, not really. We'd had to find out what 'anonymity' meant and write some examples down in our book. At least I'd done it. So I blurted out, 'It means writing something in secret, sir. Like doing a poem and not putting your name on it. Nobody knows it's you.'

'Quite so,' Mr Trewent agreed. 'So, how does that apply to the *note*.'

I read it again – and my shoulders sagged. Mrs Woolbury had forgotten to *sign* it. There was nothing to prove I hadn't written it myself. 'But, sir, Scott and Ewan can vouch for me. Honest.'

'Yessir,' sniffed Ewan. 'He spewed in the gym.'

'Delightful,' Mr Trewent said, as laughter erupted from every seat. 'Very well, Daniel. I accept your story. But before you sit down I would like to know one other example of anonymity you were able to come up with.'

'Yes, sir,' I gulped. There had only been one. 'You can make an anonymous phone call, sir.'

'Indeed you can,' Mr Trewent nodded. 'Now, go and sit down.' As I did, he repeated my answer aloud. 'Anonymous phone calls,' he boomed. 'Who can think of an instance where that might happen?'

A forest of hands went up. Oddly enough, one of them was mine. An idea had just popped into my head. An idea so strange that at first I thought it was totally cracked. Then I looked at Billy and I thought about Bushloe and slowly, very slowly, I took my hand down . . .

CHAPTER 12

'WHAT?' screeched Scott. We were down by the bike sheds. Four o'clock. I'd been working on my masterplan most of the day.

'Listen,' I said. 'Just *think* about it.'

'No way,' he said. 'It's totally mental. It's mega-ratting. It's worse than telling Crozzy.'

'*No*,' I countered. 'It's really brilliant. We want to keep Billy in the team, don't we? We just want to stop him diving, right?'

Scott looked round and didn't reply. Several other boys were coming for their bikes.

I explained my plan once more: 'If we tell Woodruff that Billy's a diver, Woodruff's going to stand off him, isn't he? Billy'll look a total prat if he hits the deck when there's no-one near him.'

Scott grimaced and shook his head in despair. 'But you can't ring a player on the *other side*.'

'But Woodruff won't know who it *is*. No-one can see you on the *phone*, can they?'

Scott shuddered and pulled his bike helmet on. 'How you gonna do it? You don't know his number.'

I slapped my hand against my brow in frustration. It was a good job one of us had a brain. 'I'll look up Woodruff in the telephone directory and find one with a Bushloe address.'

'But it's stupid. What you gonna *say* to him?'

I'd thought that through pretty carefully, of course. Over dinner, I'd written it down like a script. When he answered, I'd ask, 'Is your name Woodruff?'

'Yes,' he'd reply.

'You in Year Eight at Bushloe School?'

'Maybe. Who wants to know?'

'Doesn't matter. You're playing Willowbrook on Friday, aren't you?'

'So what?' he'd say.

'Their number nine likes to dive, that's what.'

Then I'd slam down the phone and it would all be over. From that point on it was a tactical battle between Willowbrook's striker and Bushloe's sweeper.

I explained all this to Scott.

His face took on a pained expression. 'I've got a better idea. I vote I kick Billy in the nuts in training. I owe him one for that swizz on the park.'

'Oh, brilliant,' I said, throwing up my hands. 'Our captain nobbles our striker. Very tidy. Go on, then. Do what you like. Just don't blame me if Crozzy suspends you and Hywel does you in and I die of a groin strain worrying about it. Do what you want. You're the *captain*.'

He sat back on his bike, muttering darkly. 'It's just . . . are you *sure* Woodruff won't know it's you?'

'He'd have to be a mind reader, wouldn't he?' I said.

'He is from Bushloe; they're s'posed to be smart.'

'Scotty!'

'OK, do it,' he said.

CHAPTER 13

'Someone's in a tearing rush,' said Mum, as I hurtled into the house that night.

I dropped my bag on the floor of the kitchen, jumped over Millie and dashed into the hall. 'Can I make a phone call, please?' I shouted.

'He wants to tell Marcia he loves her,' sneered Alice.

'You get on with your book,' said Mum. 'As from yesterday, the M word is banned.' She appeared at the hall door, drying a plate. 'So, have you made it up with Billy at last?'

'No,' I said, thumbing fast through the phone

book. Woodman . . . Woodrow . . . Woodruff, Woodruff, Woodruff . . . I counted twenty-four entries. Enough for an international squad! And not one of them had an address in Bushloe. 'Mum,' I asked, 'where's Bushloe near?'

'It's just off the Cottersthorpe Road,' she said.

Cottersthorpe. Of course. 'Thanks. You can go now.'

'Delighted, *your lordship*.' She did a little curtsy. 'South Pole far enough?'

Alice, meanwhile, tugged Mum's sleeve. 'I think the M word lives in Cottersthorpe,' she hissed.

'Oh Alice, shut up about the flipping M word!' Mum shooed her into the kitchen. 'Tea in five minutes,' she growled at me, then closed the door with a disgruntled thud.

There were only three Woodruffs with Cottersthorpe addresses. I started in alphabetical order: Woodruff, C., 29 Sailforth Avenue. That sounded like the sort of place a sweeper might live.

'Yes?' said a sharp male voice.

It sounded like an adult, but I couldn't be sure. I took a deep breath, closed my eyes and said, 'Can I speak to . . .' Then I realized I didn't have a name to ask for, so I put it like Mr Crozier had done, '. . . A. Woodruff, please?'

'I beg your pardon?'

'Are you A. Woodruff?'

'Yes, I'm a Woodruff,' the voice said brusquely. 'Colin Woodruff. Who is it you want?'

'*A*. Woodruff,' I stressed.

'Less of your cheek,' the voice snapped back. 'I just told you: I *am* a Woodruff. Do you want me to fetch my birth certificate or what? Here, are you one of these nuisance callers?'

'No,' I gulped.

'Well, what do you want?'

'I want a boy called Woodruff, who likes playing football, whose name begins with A – I think.'

'Well, you won't find one here,' the man replied tersely. 'There's just me and the budgie – and his name's Gordon. That begins with a G. Goodbye.' The line went dead.

'Well, you're *stupid* and that begins with an S!' I shouted, and punched in the second Cottersthorpe number.

This time I got an answering machine: 'Hi,' purred a woman's voice. 'Thanks for calling the chicks in the sticks. Julia and Joan are out right now. We're there, not here, and you're obviously not with us. So why not cheep after the beep and we'll beak a little later? Ciao for now. Here comes that beep . . .'

'Cheep, flipping cheep,' I squeaked down the phone and slammed it onto its rest again.

This wasn't at all how I'd worked it out in English. It was supposed to take less than a minute, this call. At this rate I figured I'd be here till bedtime. I heard Dad's car pulling up in the drive and quickly moved on to the last Cottersthorpe number. If Dad found out I was making lots of calls he'd definitely want to know where to and why.

I dialled again. Woodruff, N., 67 Clipperwell Drive.

'Cottersthorpe eight one four,' said a voice. Another man.

This time, I took the polite approach. 'Excuse me, do you mind if I ask you something?'

'Well, that rather depends what it is,' said the man.

'Are you Mr Woodruff?'

'Yes. Who am I speaking to, please?'

'Erm, that doesn't matter,' I faltered.

'I see,' he said, his tone becoming guarded. 'And what are you trying to sell me, exactly?'

'Pardon?'

'I've got double glazing, a fitted kitchen, the cheapest telephone rates available and I don't want a better deal on car insurance, thank you.'

'I'm not selling anything,' I spluttered. 'I just

want to know if you've got any children.'

'No, and I'm not planning to invest in any either – certainly not over the telephone. I think you have the wrong number. Goodbye.' Once again, the phone went dead.

I decided that everyone in Cottersthorpe was weird and hurled the directory across the hall – just as Dad came through.

'Hey? What's all this?' he barked.

'Nothing, OK?!'

His face turned dark. He pointed at the phone book, splayed fan-like across the bottom of the stairs. 'Pick it up, put it back and get into the kitchen. Your tea's on the table, going cold.'

'Don't want any tea.'

'Right,' he said, hanging up his coat 'Room, then, until your mood improves.'

That was fine by me. I stomped up, making the whole stairs shudder, unaware that something had fallen from my pocket. Something important.

My note from Matron.

I didn't find out until ten minutes later when Mum came in and closed the door. She settled on the bed and shook me by the shoulder. 'Danny, I want a word with you, please.'

I was lying on my stomach with my face in my pillow. 'Go away,' I sulked. I didn't want 'a word'.

'Why didn't you tell me you were sick today?'

I looked up and spotted the note in her hands. 'Forgot.'

'Is this why you're off your food tonight – or is there something more to it?'

I turned my face to the wall.

'Danny,' Mum said in a weary voice. 'What's the matter? What's going on?'

'Nothing,' I said, squirming horribly inside. I could feel a mild tweak of pain in my guts and prayed I wasn't going to heave again.

'I'm sorry, but "nothing" isn't good enough. You've been grouchier than a goat for the past few days – and now I find you were sent to Matron. If you're ill, don't you think I've got a right to know?'

I bit my lip and fought back a tear. My plan had failed. Everything had failed. We'd had it. Billy was going to be reported for diving and Willowbrook were going to be out of the Cup.

'And what's all this with the phone book?' asked Mum.

As if by magic, the telephone trilled.

'Well?' she prompted.

Feet came pounding up the stairs.

'Daniel Miller, I'm talking to you.'

Then, *wham!* Alice burst into the room.

'What?' Mum snapped.

'There's a phone call for mardy guts, I think.'

'Alice, don't talk about your brother like that. Who is it?'

'Don't know. She just wants the lad who wants to talk about football.'

I rolled over and looked Alice hard in the face.

'She?' said Mum and I together.

Alice frowned darkly. 'It's a *girl*,' she hissed.

CHAPTER 14

Suddenly, it was just like dawn had broken and brightly coloured butterflies were fluttering round the room. 'Oh,' went Mum, preening her hair. She gave me a prod. 'Well, don't keep her waiting.'

I slid off the bed and glowered at Alice.

'It's not *Marcia*,' she sneered as I clumped down the stairs.

Which got me wondering – who could it be? I'd never had a phone call from a girl in my life. 'Hello?' I said in a nervous whisper.

'OK, this is gonna sound weird,' she said.

Too right. She didn't sound like anyone I'd ever met.

'My Uncle Colin,' she blabbed on regardless, 'just rang up and said there was this barmy kid – that's you, by the way – ringing round trying to find someone called Woodruff who likes football. Is that right?'

'Er, yeah,' I said, a bit confused. My head felt like it was filling up with bubble bath.

'I think he dialled that code,' she went on. 'The one you can do to get the last person's number – fourteen seventy something or other; it's the year that Ivan the Third took Novgorod.'

'What?'

'Ivan the Third,' she said. 'We're doing it this term in *History Can Be Fun*. Anyway, my Uncle Colin, being a brainy sort of bloke, passed your number on to me 'cos he thought I might know who it was you wanted. Am I making sense?'

'I think so,' I said.

'Great. Here I am, then. Whaddya want?'

Miraculously, some of the soap bubbles popped. If I understood this girl correctly, she had the surname Woodruff. In which case . . . 'Have you got a brother?' I blurted.

'Two,' she sniffed. 'Unfortunately.'

I felt my shoulders stiffen. 'Do they both go to Bushloe School?'

'Yep,' she said. 'Why, where do you go.'

'Nowhere,' I said.

'Nowhere?' she repeated. 'You've gotta go somewhere.'

Which nearly made me slam down the phone. Maybe ringing Woodruff *was* too risky. It was the scariest thing I'd ever done in my life. It didn't help that I had to talk to his sister. I raised the phone to my mouth again. 'You know your brothers, do they like football?'

''Course!' she exclaimed. 'Who do you support?'

'Liverpool,' I muttered, anxiously aware that we'd veered off the subject.

'Hmm, totally predictable,' she said. 'Still, they're not bad, I s'pose. They're not Swansea, like, but it could have been worse. Do you play?'

'Pardon?'

'Footie: do you play?'

'Erm . . . yeah.' Who *was* this girl?

'What position?'

'Midfield.'

'Centre or wing-back?'

'Roving,' I said.

'Like Jamie Redknapp?'

'He doesn't play for Liverpool now.'

'Yeah, I know,' she said, and giggled slightly. 'Don't s'pose you look like Jamie, do you?'

I furrowed my brow. 'Why do you want to know that?'

'Just something I'm doing for a project,' she

muttered. 'Hang on, Mum's calling.' There was a clunk as she laid the receiver down. In the background I heard a woman's voice hiss: 'Mandy, will you please get off that phone? This chicken supreme you were so desperate for me to cook is starting to look like chicken sludge.'

'Put a dish on it,' Mandy replied through her teeth. 'I can't come now, Mum, I'm talking to a boy about Jamie Redknapp.' She swung the phone back up to her mouth. 'Sorry, Mum's giving me grief as usual.'

'Don't think I didn't hear that, madam!'

'Please,' I said, getting a bit desperate. 'I just want to talk to—'

'What's your name?' she cut in suddenly.

'Danny,' I said, gritting my teeth.

'I'm Mandy,' she said. 'Horrible, isn't it?'

'Better than *Alice*,' I said. I could see her craning her neck over the banister. Her ears were the size of water-lilies.

'Alice?' said Mandy. 'She your girlfriend?'

'No, she's my horrible *baby* sister.' Stung by this slur, Alice stuck out her tongue. I willed her to topple downstairs, but she didn't.

'Better than having two brothers,' said Mandy.

'Yeah,' I jumped in, as her mum piped up: 'Amanda Woodruff! Do I have to come and *drag* you off that phone?'

'*Mum, keep your wig on! I'm coming, OK?* Sorry, gotta go,' she breathed down the line. 'Ta for ringing. I could talk to you all night.'

'You rang me,' I reminded her.

'Oh yeah,' she giggled. 'What about? It's been ages.'

'I want to talk to your brother,' I snapped. At last, in all the babble, I'd got it out.

'Oh yeah, right. I'll see if he's in. *Dean!*' she screamed at the top of her voice.

Dean? Maybe I'd got the wrong house after all?'

'Went out ten minutes ago,' Mrs Woodruff shouted. 'Same as the gas on my flipping oven.'

'Gone out, sorry,' Mandy replied. 'Do you want me to give him a message for you?'

'No,' I said. 'Is your other brother in?'

'Adam?' she said. 'You want to talk to Adam?'

Adam. Yes. He had to be the one. 'Please,' I breathed, quivering a little.

I sensed her give a gentle shrug. 'OK,' she peeped. 'I think he's playing out—'

But before she could finish, Mrs Woodruff wrestled the phone from her grip. 'I'm sorry, Mr Redknapp, or whoever you are, my daughter is engaged to have tea right now.'

'*Mum, will you please let go of that phone!*'

'As you have discovered, she can talk the hind legs off every donkey from here to Prestatyn. She has also forfeited her pocket money in telephone charges and is barred from making any more calls.'

'*Oh, Mum. That is so embarrassing!*'

'So lovely to chat to you. Bye now.'

Click.

CHAPTER 15

It took a few moments for the horror to sink in. I had come within *seconds* of completing my mission, only for some mum to interfere as usual! My own mum came down the stairs just then (Alice like an evil assistant in her shadow).

'OK?' she chirped, trying to sound cheerful, hoping to discover who the *girl* was, probably.

'No,' I snapped. 'What year did Ivan the Third take Novlinod?'

'Eh?' she said, blinking in surprise. It was hardly the answer she'd been expecting. She glanced at Alice.

'He's crackers,' said Alice.

Not crackers, desperate. I just *had* to get Mandy back on the phone. And the only quick way was to find that code, the one her Uncle Colin had dialled to get my number.

'It might be Nobblibog!' I shouted, rushing into the dining room in search of a suitable encyclopaedia.

'Danny, what are you on about?' said Mum.

But I was already tearing through the reference books, looking up entries for Ivan the Third – when, unexpectedly, the phone rang again. I burst into the hall and yanked up the receiver. 'Mandy?'

'That Danny?'

'Yes!'

'It's Marcia.'

'Marcia?' My stomach contracted to the size of a walnut.

Alice fell flat against the door in shock. Even Mum raised a rather startled eyebrow. She tugged Alice's sleeve. Together they tiptoed back upstairs.

'Williams,' added Marcia. 'You've not forgotten me already?'

'No,' I gulped. 'What do you want?'

'Oh, very enchanting,' she sang. 'Not, "How are you, Marcia?" or "Nice to hear from you, Marcia," but "Whaddya want?" Very cordial, *not*.'

'Sorry,' I whimpered.

'All right, you're forgiven – but only 'cos I want a favour, like. I can't find Robert the Bruce.'

'Uh?' I grunted, totally confused.

'I've lost page two of my history essay. I nearly had to stay behind because of you. Miss Peet didn't believe that a great Scottish nobleman could have been abducted by a boy in Year Eight.'

'Pardon?'

She let out a weary sigh. 'When you got bumped by those juniors this morning, I dropped some of my stuff too. You must have picked up my essay by mistake. Do you think you could run away and look for it, please?'

I dropped the phone instantly and hurried to my bag. Sure enough, sandwiched between some clean sheets of graph paper and a page of fantasy football elevens was a neatly written piece of Scottish history. I dashed it back to the phone. 'Found it!'

'Phew. My hero.'

That made me blush from head to toe. Then suddenly, I had a bold idea. 'Marcia, can I ask you something, please?'

'My, this sounds interesting,' she purred.

'Are you good at history?'

'Not bad, I s'pose.' Now she sounded slightly disappointed.

'Do you know about Ivan the Third?'

'*Who?*'

So I told her everything Mandy had said – as much as I could remember, anyway.

'You mean one four seven one?' she guessed. 'That's the code you dial to hear the number of the last person who called.'

'Oh, *brilliant*!' I gasped, scribbling it down. 'Thanks, Marcia! You're totally ace!'

At the top of the stairs, Alice gasped in shock. She pounded along the landing to Mum.

I just pinked all the way to my socks.

'Ace,' Marcia repeated.

'S-sorry,' I mumbled. 'I didn't mean . . .'

There was a frosty silence from somewhere in Cottersthorpe. When she did speak again, she took me by surprise: 'Who's Mandy?' she asked.

'No-one,' I whispered, biting my lip. For some strange reason I felt horribly guilty, talking to Marcia about another girl.

'You said her name when you answered the phone. She your girlfriend, then?'

'Haven't got a girlfriend,' I murmured.

There was a pause, then Marcia said really coolly: 'Do you fancy me, Daniel Miller?'

My stomach flipped like a tossed pancake. What was I supposed to say to that? If I said 'no' she'd probably explode; if I said 'yes' *I'd* probably explode. 'A bit,' I gulped.

'Only a *bit*?'

'I mean loads,' I blurted. 'I think you're really . . . pretty.'

Trust Dad to appear in the doorway then. He coughed into his fist and tactfully retreated. I squirmed in embarrassment and stamped my foot. There was a humming sound at Marcia's end. I could picture her holding the phone on her shoulder, swinging her bobbed hair, breathing on her nails. Suddenly she said, 'You haven't forgotten that swap of ours, have you?'

'No,' I said, trembling.

'Good,' she chirped. 'It was special, wasn't it, that book I gave you?'

'Yes,' I said (depending how you looked at it).

'So that deserves a special swap, right?'

'Yes,' I breathed. What was she after?

'So, is there anything *special* you'd like to ask me – apart from peculiar history questions?'

'Erm . . .' I floundered.

'Oh, lads, you're all so useless,' she said. 'OK, I'll make it easy for you: would you like to meet me on the park, tonight?'

'What for?' I muttered, touching my groin, suddenly feeling queasy again.

'A *date*, idiot. Seven o'clock. On the seats by the pond. And don't turn up in your uniform or you're chucked. Bring my essay with you, OK?'

'OK,' I squeaked.

'See you later, then. Bye.'

'Bye,' I gulped, and put the phone down.

And two seconds later, yakked all over it.

CHAPTER 16

'YEUCCHH!' went Alice when she saw what I'd done. She pinched her nose and grimaced at Mum.

I thought Mum would go into orbit. Instead, she just looked very concerned. 'Disinfectant and a cloth,' she said quietly to Alice. She pulled a tissue from her sleeve and wiped my mouth. 'Bed,' she said. I wasn't going to argue. My shoulders were as cold as two lumps of ice.

As I took the first step Dad looked into the hall. 'What the—?'

Mum held up a hand and cut him off. 'Young love, it's a wonderful thing,' she said.

Dad just sighed and left her to it.

Fifteen minutes of phone cleaning later, Mum came up and sat on my bed. This time, I'd crawled right under the duvet, just my shorts and T-shirt on.

'Well,' she said, 'here we are again.' Only now her voice was gentle and caring. She parted my fringe and ran a knuckle down my cheek. 'Are you ready to tell me about this yet?' She pointed to my tummy.

I shuddered slightly. This time I knew I would have to give an answer. So I told her how I'd yakked in the gym.

'I bet that pleased Mr Crozier,' she said.

'He said it was nerves, about the next game.'

She nodded once, then her gaze flicked up. 'So how does that explain what happened downstairs? It didn't sound like you were discussing the offside rule with Marcia.'

'Mu-um,' I tutted. 'You shouldn't have been listening.'

'I wasn't; I've got a good spy, remember?'

Hmph. Alice. The sister from Wonderland, not.

'All right,' Mum said, sparing my blushes. 'I'm not going to pry into your private life. But your health and welfare *is* my business; I don't want you vomiting over any more household objects, thank you. Something's obviously not right inside

106

and the best thing you can do for now is rest. Let's see how you are in the morning. You've probably just picked up a mild tummy bug.'

'Probably,' I said. I wasn't going to tell her about my strain.

'Oh, by the way, I got this for you.' She held up a note from the telephone pad. 'You wrote down one four seven one, so I assumed you were after the last person who called. It *was* this Marcia girl, wasn't it?'

I slapped my hands to my face in frustration. 'No-oo,' I moaned. 'I want *Mandy*, not Marcia!'

'Mandy?' Mum repeated, frowning hard. She looked as if she'd suffered a bout of amnesia and had somehow missed out on half of my life.

I ignored her and punched my pillow. 'I hate Billy Peters! I hate him. I hate him. And ducks. And rhubarb. And Damien Clegge!'

'Hang on,' said Mum. 'Now I'm really lost. Who's Damien Clegge? And what's rhubarb got to do with it? Did you have that for dinner? That can make you ill if it's not cooked properly.'

'Billy Peters is worse than a spot on the bum!'

'Lovely,' said Mum. 'I'll tell his mother next time I see her.'

I buried my face in my pillow.

Mum patted her thighs and rose to leave. She seemed to have accepted that she wasn't going to get much sense from me tonight. 'Sweet dreams,' she said tiredly. 'Shout if you need me.'

'Don't need *anyone*.'

'Brain surgeon?' she muttered, and closed the door.

Whichever way I twisted, I couldn't get to sleep. My mind was overflowing with Billy and Adam; Adam and Billy; like a mental tug-of-war. When I did drop off I dreamed about football. Willowbrook v. Bushloe in the World Cup Final. One all in extra time. Bryan Pringle, and my dad, were commentating on the game . . .

'*One minute to go,*' Bryan Pringle jabbered, '*and Miller knocks a high ball into the area. Woodruff and Peters both go up for it and – oh my goodness! Peters hits the deck. Now, was he brought down? Yes! The referee's given a penalty! Well, I have to say that's very harsh. It looked like a perfectly good challenge to me.*'

'He dived, Bryan,' my dad chipped in. '*Peters has wrapped young Woodruff up a treat and posted him first-class into the bargain. It's ruining the game, this play-acting lark. It's about time someone made a stand.*'

'It looks like someone might be,' Bryan Pringle continued. '*There's an awful kerfuffle going on on the pitch. Miller and Peters are having a right ding-dong. Miller is refusing to take the penalty and telling Peters* to quack off, I think. Uh-oh, now Miller's uprooted a stick of rhubarb from a little patch growing by the corner flag and he's chasing Peters round the goal-mouth with it.'

'Miller's got a card as well, now, Bryan.'

'Yes, while all that was going on, Mr Crozieri, the Italian referee, has shown Danny Miller the yellow card for time wasting and told him to get on with taking this penalty. So, here is Miller, the boy who's never missed a penalty in his life. He runs in now and . . . goodness, skips right over the ball! What on earth is Miller doing? Hang on, he's turned in the six-yard box. He's running back to the ball again . . . he's struck the ball with phenomenal power towards his own goal! And . . . it's over the head of Thomas and in! Miller has scored an own goal from the opposing penalty spot. What do you make of that, Dad?'

'Stupid, Bryan, but incredibly sporting.'

'Well, the crowd clearly agree. They're chanting Miller's name all round the ground. Woodruff comes up and shakes Miller's hand. And here's Miller's girlfriend on the pitch as well: teenage supermodel, Marcia Williams. She throws her arms round Miller's neck . . .'

'Danny!'

Miller puckers his lips.

'Wake up, rat face!'

He draws her in close.

'Danny, get off me!'

Miller gives her an enormous smacker!

'UGGGGH!' screamed a shrill little voice. Something struggled in my arms. Something that wasn't Marcia Williams. I opened my eyes and there was . . .

'ALICE!' I squealed and sat up, banging my head on my lamp.

'I hate you! I hate you! I HATE you!' she stamped, scrubbing her mouth with the sleeve of her jumper. 'I'm NEVER coming to wake you EVER again! Mum! Danny *kissed* me! On the lips. And it was WET!' She pounded to the bathroom.

Mum pounded upstairs. 'Danny?' she said. 'What on earth's going on? Why is Alice . . .' she looked into the bathroom, '. . . gargling with mouthwash?'

I pulled up the duvet and didn't reply.

'Never mind,' Mum sighed, too rushed to bother. 'How are you this morning? Any more sickness?'

I gave a little shrug. In truth, there was a strange sort of aching in my tummy. I figured it was either one of two things: love-pangs for Marcia or disgust at the thought of snogging Alice. I quaked and Mum instantly pounced on it. 'Are you hurting? Down here?' She laid a hand across her groin.

'A bit,' I grimaced.

She rose to her feet. 'Right, that's it. I think you

might have a grumbling appendix. I'm going to give Dr Hamer a call.'

What?! I sat up like a prairie dog. 'Mum, I'm not going to Dr Hamer's!'

'You don't have to, silly; he'll come here.'

'He can't. It's Tuesday. You're at work and I'm at school.'

She paused to think. 'I'll switch my shift. Anyway, if I tell the surgery it's a possible emergency, Dr Hamer will come out within the hour.'

'EMERGENCY?!'

'Calm *down*,' she tutted. 'You might strain something.' She pressed on my shoulders and forced me into bed. 'I won't be happy till this is checked out. You're staying put and that's final, Danny.'

'Mum, *please*. I've *got* to go to school. If Mr Crozier thinks I'm ill, he'll drop me from the team.'

'No arguments,' she said. 'Your health is more important than a football match. I'll be back when I've packed your sister off to school.'

Appropriately, Alice stormed out of the bathroom. 'You're DEAD!' she yelled, going past my door.

Mum sighed and shook her head in dismay. She scooped a few items of clothing off the floor and hurried downstairs, shouting after Alice.

I bounced a slipper off the door in protest. I

couldn't *believe* it had come to this. Never mind the guilt and the worry and the vomit, now I might have a grumbling appendix! And all because of what?

Billy quacking Peters!

CHAPTER 17

Worst of all, I'd jilted Marcia. It only occurred to me when the doorbell rang that I'd totally forgotten our meeting on the park.

I was in a cold sweat when the doctor came in. 'My, you do look pale,' he said.

He would be, too, if he'd just stood up the best girl in school.

Mum poured out a list of my symptoms.

'Mmm,' went the doctor, feeling my groin, making me wince in the region of my pull.

'How is he?' Mum asked. She put a hand to her chest.

Dr Hamer pulled up my bottoms. 'Hmm. Fine – for now.'

That sounded ominous. 'I've got to play Bushloe on Friday,' I squeaked.

'Oh, you'll be fit for Friday,' he muttered.

I flopped against my pillow with a sigh of relief.

The doctor smiled and closed his bag. 'Nothing much to worry about, Mrs Miller. The vomiting, as you say, is probably little more than a mild tummy bug combined, perhaps, with nerves about the match. Plenty of fluids should clear it out. His appendix, however, is a wee bit tender. We'll have to keep a watchful eye on that. I'd like to see him again in a few weeks' time. If we do have to snip it, we'll try and arrange it for the cricket season, shall we?' He gave me a wink and sprang to his toes.

'Excuse me,' I called. 'Can I go to school? It's Games this afternoon. Training – for Friday.'

Dr Hamer paused by the door. 'Tomorrow,' he said. 'Give Games a miss. You don't have to stay in bed, but train with a jigsaw or something today.'

Jigsaw? Big help. That would really keep me fit. But Mum took the doctor at his word.

'Zebras?' I protested.

'It's a good one,' she said, clearing a space on the front-room table. 'Two thousand pieces. Haven't done it in ages.' She opened the box and a landslide of black and white stripes poured forth.

114

'Look on the bright side. We don't often get the chance to spend time alone together. It's a perfect opportunity to chat.'

'What about?'

Her eyebrows narrowed. 'There's no need to sound so defensive,' she tutted. She turned to the jigsaw again. 'You could start by unravelling the rhubarb mystery. I spent hours trying to work that out last night. It was worse than having a pip between my teeth.'

'You wouldn't understand,' I muttered.

She pushed a piece of straight-edged sky my way. 'Try me,' she said.

So, reluctantly, I did. I told her all about the *Strike Hard* video and what had happened after the Cuff Lane match.

'Fight?' she exclaimed. 'You and Billy? But you've always been as happy as hamsters before.'

'It's his fault,' I said, arranging the corner bits. 'It wouldn't have happened if he hadn't bought that video.'

'Oh, Danny.' She reached over and squeezed my hand. 'I understand what you're saying, and I admire you for wanting the team to play fairly. But what Billy does is not your concern. You should play *your* game, the best you can, even if someone in the side *is* cheating.'

'But what if he does something really bad,

115

Mum? What if he gets another boy sent off or we get booted out of the Cup?' I told her about the notebook then, and Bryan Pringle's article on diving.

She frowned mildly and stirred some bits. 'Have you talked to Mr Crozier?'

'He knows,' I said. 'He told Billy he had to stop diving, but Billy just said he wasn't doing it.'

Mum joined her hands in her lap. 'Well, if it was me, I would go back and talk to Billy. I'd tell him, without getting stroppy, that I was very unhappy about what he's doing and that he's a good enough player already without having to resort to this . . . video nasty.'

I shook my head. 'He won't listen, Mum. He feels dead important. He thinks he's winning the games for us.'

'Well, in that case, you just have to let things be. The situation will sort itself out. He'll get his come-uppance, one way or another.'

'Yes, Mum,' I said with a heavy sigh. I knew she meant well, but what if it was the *team* that got its come-uppance?

'Anyway,' she said, testing a piece of African plain against the nearest water hole, 'forget about blooming football for a moment. At the risk of getting my head bitten off – this Mandy girl, where does she fit in?'

'Nowhere. She's just . . . a girl,' I said. I didn't want to tell Mum the reason for my phone call. I had the feeling she might not approve of my plan.

'Well, tell me about her. What's she like?'

'Dunno. She's OK. She blabs on a bit.'

'Well, that's not very endearing, is it?'

'Mum, I've not gone *soft* on her.'

She flashed me a look. 'Well, you could have fooled me. The way you were beating your pillow last night it was almost as if she was the last girl on the planet.'

I squirmed and made an awkward face.

'All right. What about the other M word? Marcia? You're not two-timing, are you?'

'Mum!'

'I'm only *asking*,' she stressed.

'You said that the M word was banned.'

'Oh, that was just to keep Alice quiet.'

'I hate Alice,' I muttered. 'Can't we give her away?'

'Don't be horrible. Alice loves you, very much indeed. In fact, right now, I'd say she's secretly rather proud of you.'

'Pff! You're *kidding*?'

We both looked down at the jigsaw box. A fine spray of spit now lay across it. Mum wiped it clean with a rub of her elbow. 'Don't spit across the picture, there's a good lad. It rarely rains in this part of Africa.'

I forced a smile. 'Why would Alice be proud of me?'

'Isn't it obvious? Her brother's only chatting up the best-looking girl in school, by all accounts.'

'Hmph, not for much longer,' I muttered. I told her about 'the date' that wasn't.

'Oh, Danny,' she scolded. 'Why didn't you say? You should never let a girl down like that. I had her number. I could have phoned her for you.'

I looked away, red-faced. 'I just forgot.'

She shook her head. 'That's a poor excuse. Well, I hope you've got a decent ladder, because the next time you see Miss Marcia Williams you're going to have quite a hole to climb out of.'

'Essay!' I shouted, jumping up and pranging my knees on the table.

'Pardon?' said Mum. 'How on earth did we get from holes to essays?'

I shot a glance at the clock. Nine forty exactly. Assembly was over ten minutes ago. I'd forgotten *Marcia's essay*. Now I was really cooked. 'Mum, I've got to go to school, *right now*. Marcia will go totally spare if I don't.' I told her all about Robert the Bruce.

Mum sighed like a wounded animal. 'Talk about "always in the mire, only the depth varies".

All right, I'll ring the school and explain what's happened. You're not going in with a grumbling appendix. Even Marcia will understand that.'

'But, Mum . . .'

'Danny, no. I don't care how gorgeous this girl is, you're staying put. That's an order.'

So I tried a different approach. '*You* could take it in; on your way to work.'

She looked at me askance. 'Danny, I'm not *going* to work; I'm staying here, looking after my love-struck son.'

'But you *could* go, Mum. You don't start till ten. And you're always saying how much they need you. You can make it in time if you drive really fast.'

'I—' she began, but I cut her off again.

'I'll be all right on my own, honest.' I stuck out my tongue and made a healthy-sounding 'Aah!'

'No,' she said, leaning back in her seat.

'Please,' I begged. 'Please, Mum, *please*. It'd be a good way of making it up to her, wouldn't it?'

She flicked me a searching look, then switched her gaze to the mantelpiece clock. 'Well . . .'

'Aw, thanks, Mum!' I threw my arms round her neck.

'All right,' she said. 'On one condition. I'll take your essay into school, but I want to meet this Marcia girl. When you're back on speaking terms, invite her round for tea. Is that a deal?'

My throat went dry. My grin went limp. Invite Marcia round? I'd probably melt before the words could leave my lips.

Mum squeezed past me and hurried to the kitchen, grabbing her bag and keys along the way. 'Call me at the shop if you start to feel bad. Do you promise, faithfully, to look after yourself?'

'Yes,' I grunted.

'Open a can of soup for your dinner. And no training when I'm gone. No press-ups. Or bunny jumps.'

'Hops,' I corrected her. 'Can I go for a walk? Just round the cricket pitch? I'll be bored if I stay in the house all day.'

She reappeared, pulling a brush through her hair. 'No. Well – all right. But not far. You can do me a favour and post this letter.' She opened her bag and put a sealed white envelope in my hands. 'Make sure it's in the box for the one o'clock collection. It's important. Don't forget.'

'OK,' I said, and glanced at the address:

Ms W. B. Arrowsmith
11 Medlars Road
Cottersthorpe
Nr. Bushloe

'And don't be out long.'

Cottersthorpe . . . Nr. Bushloe . . .

'Danny, are you listening?'

My heart began to pound. *'Bushloe,'* I murmured.

'Umm?' Mum said, biting on a hair grip.

'Nothing,' I gulped, and put the letter aside.

She kissed the tip of her finger and tapped me on the nose. 'First twinge of pain – you call me, OK?'

'OK,' I nodded.

'Bye, then.'

'Bye.'

And that was that. With a wave she was gone. Leaving me alone with my thoughts.

And that letter.

HALF-TIME INTERVAL

I should have ignored it right from the start. As soon as the idea came into my head I should have gone racing after Mum, plopped the letter back into her hands and said: 'Sorry, Mum, I might strain my appendix reaching up to the letterbox. Better post this letter yourself, after all.'

Then nothing would have happened the way it did.

But I didn't go racing after Mum. As soon as her car pulled off the drive, I picked up the letter and looked at it again. In a flash, a little devil jumped onto my shoulder . . .

Psst! I've got a great idea! it hissed.

'Go away,' I said, trying feebly to resist.

You know that letter? the little devil pressed.

'Yeah, what about it?'

You could bike up to Bushloe and post it yourself.

I shuddered so much I almost fell off my chair.

And while you're there . . .

'Oh yeah,' I muttered, staring out of the window, 'that's the worst idea I've ever heard.'

The little devil snickered mischievously: *So how come you're looking for the map, then, eh?*

It was terrible, like being on auto-pilot, driven by a force I couldn't control. I reached over to the bookcase and pulled out a map of the local district. I opened it out on the front-room floor, turning it once to get my bearings. Cottersthorpe Road, running through Willowbrook, Cottersthorpe and Disley. I let my finger travel along it, following a fork that led north – to Bushloe. And there, on the edge of Bushloe Park, right alongside the river Willow, was the little set of marks I was looking for: Bushloe School.

Twenty minutes on a bike, the little devil sniffed.

'Twenty-five,' I said.

You're the boss, it replied.

'But, I *can't*,' I moaned, pushing the map away. 'What if Mum . . . ?'

Stay cool, the little devil simpered. *Mum's at work*

till three, remember. And even if she did find out you'd gone, you've got the perfect excuse.

'What?' I said.

You were so engrossed with doing the jigsaw you forgot to keep an eye on the clock. And dear, oh dear, by the time you'd remembered about your errand you'd missed the post. Then you thought that Mum would be cross. So you got on your bike, rode up to Bushloe and delivered her letter yourself, by hand. She did say it was important, didn't she? Meanwhile, you start on the other letter.

'Other letter?' I muttered nervously.

The one you're going to write to Adam, said the voice.

I lay on my back and thought it through. In some ways, a letter was better than the phone. I couldn't stumble over my words in a letter, and I could still be anonymous as well. If I went up to Bushloe at dinnertime, there were bound to be loads of kids about. All I had to do was find a boy of my age and ask him to pass on a letter to Adam. Everyone in Adam's year would know him. Then, when the job was done, I could whizz off up to Medlars Road, post Mum's letter and come home. Sorted.

Only one thing bothered me: what if I stopped a bunch of kids and one of them turned out to be

Adam himself? What if I met the Bushloe super-star, face to face, outside the gates of his school? It was a pretty slim chance but it *could* just happen. The last thing I wanted was an awkward scene, three days before we met on the pitch.

That's why I decided to go in disguise.

I checked myself out in the long hall mirror. I had my Liverpool cap pulled down really tight and Dad's mirrored sunglasses hiding my eyes. I even tried on the false moustache I'd got with a conjuring kit one Christmas.

I lifted a finger and pointed at the glass. 'You don't know me,' I told my reflection, 'and you'll never see me again, OK?'

Miaow, went Millie, choosing that moment to use my leg as a scratching post.

'Ow!' I yelled and doubled up in pain. The moustache fell off. As I scrambled to retrieve it, the shades went too. I should have known then it was a warning sign.

Don't go, Danny. Stay at home, son.

But my mind was one big blur of adventure.

I slipped the shades back on and patted my pocket. Inside were two identical envelopes, one of them my letter to Adam Woodruff.

Beware of the Willowbrook duck

it said, in carefully pasted newspaper print. There was even a picture of a plastic duck I'd cut out from one of Alice's books. I'd done a speech bubble coming from the duck's mouth, too:

I was pretty sure Adam would guess what it meant. With my left hand, I scrawled on the front of the envelope:

For A.Woodruff-from a friend

I licked the flap twice and sealed it down. Then I went for my bike.

SECOND HALF

SECOND HALF

CHAPTER
1

In the past I'd often heard Dad complain about traffic jams and roadworks on the journey through Cottersthorpe. But I whizzed along in top gear most of the way and was bumping down the cycle tracks on Bushloe Park well within my estimated twenty-five minutes. I saw the school buildings right away: three old-fashioned red-brick blocks, not quite hidden by a wall of trees. A spidery trail of black-hooped railings marked the periphery of the main school grounds. Straight ahead was the rear of the kitchens. A door was open and a tall thin woman in a blue checked hat was clanking a trolley-load of aluminium containers. Steam was billowing out of a window. There was a dreadful smell of fish in the air. It was dinnertime at Bushloe High, for sure.

Suddenly, away to the right, I heard the faint sound of a whistle being blown. I turned at once in the direction of the peep and saw a wide expanse of playing fields. Two football teams, one in yellow bibs, the other in blue, were jogging in parallel lines past a goalmouth. I pedalled furiously towards them. Never mind the letter, wouldn't it be something to catch sight of the Bushloe mid-school eleven out on a pre-Cup training session? I could analyse their team formation, their dead-ball moves, their—

'Oi, watch out!'

With a screech, I had to brake hard and fast as two boys met me head-on around a bend. My front wheel swerved away to the left, nearly sending me into a hedge. I grabbed a railing hoop and steadied myself.

'Aw, look at this!' one boy moaned. He pulled a tissue from his pocket and dabbed at an orange stain on his shirt. The shock of the near-collision had made him smack a lolly against his chest. 'You're not s'posed to bike round here, you know.'

His mate, a long-faced, toothy kid, pointed a

bony finger at the ground. A white 'stick' figure had been painted on the path.

'Sorry,' I muttered. 'I'm new round here. I'm ... looking for someone.' And this pair could help. They were wearing the bottle-green Bushloe blazers. More importantly, they looked my age. 'Do you know a boy called Adam Woodruff?'

They looked at one another. 'No,' they said.

'What year are you in?'

'Eight,' they admitted.

'You must know him, then. He's dead good at football.'

They shrugged as if football came a long way down their list of interests. The boy with the lolly picked his nose. 'Why have you got those sunglasses on?'

'When it's not even sunny?' his mate chipped in.

That raised a nervous gulp in my throat, but I wasn't going to show it, not in front of these two. 'Which way is it to the school gates?' I asked.

'That way,' they said, pointing in completely opposite directions.

'Thanks,' I said. Very helpful, not.

The boy with the lolly looked at his mate. 'He's cracked,' he muttered, and they shuffled away.

'Don't care, we're gonna stuff you on Friday,' I whispered, and pedalled on the way I'd been heading (over as many stick-figures as I could find).

Before long I had exited the park and come upon a dappled country lane. The lane twisted and dropped for another hundred metres, before levelling out past a little row of shops. Kids in green jackets were dotted all about. A bunch of them were grouped around a newsagent's shop, sitting on a low wall, sipping drinks. I stood on the pedals and freewheeled towards them, hanging hard left (and school-side) for the moment. As I bumped onto the pavement, I found myself looking at a large, square playground. There was a female teacher on duty nearby. She was wearing a blousy yellow anorak and marching up and down, clapping her hands behind her back. She clocked me the moment I trundled past. A cloud of suspicion swept over her face. I could sense her thinking: What's that boy doing out of uniform and riding a bike around here, at this time? Why isn't he in school? That on its own was bad enough. But in the second it had taken to exchange a glance, another, more worrying thought had surfaced: I had the prickly feeling I'd seen her before.

For one panic-stricken moment I thought about turning round and running. But how could I know her? Or she know me? She was from Bushloe; I was from Willowbrook. Even so, I wasn't going to take any chances. I rode the bike out of the teacher's sight and rested it against the back of a bench. A studious-looking boy, about my age, eyed me suspiciously and pushed his stubby nose deep into a book. I sat down beside him.

''Scuse me,' I whispered. 'Can I talk to you a minute?'

His feet shifted anxiously against the pavement. 'Don't want any stuff,' he said.

'Stuff?' I repeated.

He pulled away, like a crab going into its shell. 'We've had films, you know. About people selling drugs.'

'I'm not a drug dealer,' I snapped, drawing stares from several kids, including a group of girls across the road.

'What do you want, then?' the boy went on. 'If you show me any tablets, I'll call a teacher.'

'Are you in Year Eight?'

He gave a hesitant nod.

'Do you know a boy called Adam Woodruff?'

'Who?' he said, looking puzzled.

'Woodruff,' I repeated.

There was a pause while he thought about it. 'Ask her,' he said, thrusting out an arm. And he pointed vaguely at the group of girls. One of them, a dopey-looking kid with freckles, gave her mate an urgent nudge.

'Don't *you* know?' I said, turning back to the boy. Only to find he had snapped his book shut and cleared off back to the safety of the yard.

I ground my teeth in desperation. Now, it seemed, I had only one choice.

I rolled my bike towards the girls. Freckle-face hooked her finger in her mouth. 'Cheryl,' she hissed. 'Look what's coming.'

A girl sipping cola turned my way. She eyed me up and down and the straw fell off her lip. 'Donna,' she whispered. 'Check this out.'

Donna, a dark-haired, gum-chewing girl, said, 'Shut up, Trace. We're doing boy-talk here. Go on, then,' she asked the fourth in the group, a girl on the wall whose face was hidden by Donna's body. 'How long have you been going with him?'

The girl responded with a tired snort. 'Donna, I *told* you. I'm not going with him. We're just . . . y'know, mates.'

Donna gave a sniff and folded her arms. 'You're mates with a boy who looks like—?'

'Excuse me,' I cut in sheepishly, leaning my bike against a bin. The conversation stopped abruptly. All four of them looked my way. Cheryl took a timid slurp of cola. Donna gave a cocky tilt of her head. Tracey bit a knuckle and started to giggle. The fourth girl's gaze travelled straight to my cap.

'This him?' said Donna. 'Come to see you?' She uncrossed her arms. 'Take your glasses off. Go on.'

'Why?' I mumbled, glancing around.

'I want to see if you look like – what'shisname again?'

And suddenly I knew who the fourth girl was. 'Mandy?' I spluttered.

'Danny?' she gasped. She pushed herself off the wall to stand a good ten centimetres taller than the others. She stared at me with wide blue eyes. I couldn't stop looking at her mountain of hair. She had what Mum would call a 'pineapple cut' – tons of the stuff, bunched up at the back, bits frizzing off like a fireworks display.

'Get his hat,' Donna ordered.

Tracey jumped forward and snatched my cap.

'Oi!' I cried. She passed it to Cheryl, who passed it to Donna.

'Tch,' went Donna, wrinkling her nose. 'He doesn't look a bit like Jamie Fing-fang.'

'Nice bum, though,' said Tracey, stepping side-ways.

Cheryl giggled fiercely and chewed her hair.

'What's he doing here?' Donna asked Mandy.

Mandy pushed forward and looped my arm.

'I want to give a message to Adam,' I hissed.

She pulled me quickly away from the others. 'In a minute. Do this first, OK?'

'Do what?' I said.

She turned me to face her. 'Honestly, Danny,'

she announced out loud, 'why didn't you *say* you were coming to see me?'

'I wasn't,' I said.

She pinched my arm and turned coyly to her mates. 'You can brag all you like about lads, Donna Plummer, but you've never been with one from *another school*, have you? Excuse me. No looking, now.'

'She's never?' said Tracey.

'Is too,' gasped Cheryl.

'Tart,' sniffed Donna, as Mandy pressed her warm lips hard against mine.

'Don't struggle,' she said, without moving away, which made it look like a *real* snog.

'Cor,' said Tracey. 'That's not bad. Do you think he used his tongue?'

'Hmph,' went Donna, picking her nails.

Cheryl gulped and squashed her can.

'Thanks,' Mandy whispered, letting me go. She touched her fingers against my chest. 'Thanks, Danny. I owe you one. Why don't you take your glasses off? You *are* Danny, aren't you?'

It seemed a bit late to be asking me *that*. But I wasn't going to stand there and argue with her. All I wanted now was out. I pulled an envelope from my pocket and slapped it in her hand. 'Give this to Adam. Don't tell him who sent it.'

She glanced at the envelope. 'But—?' she started.

'I've gotta go,' I said, and snatched up my bike.

'Tch, love you and leave you,' sniffed Donna.

'Danny, wait!' cried Mandy, grabbing hold of the handlebars.

'Let go,' I snapped, acutely aware that girls *and* boys were circling us now. I pressed on a pedal. The wheels didn't turn. Mandy was very much stronger than she looked.

'Stop,' she pleaded, 'you don't understand. There's no point giving this letter to Adam.'

'Look out,' I heard someone hiss. I knew that tone. It was a warning cry. Teacher coming! Panicking, I wrenched the handlebars aside and managed to throw Mandy slightly off balance.

'What's going on there?' a woman's voice shouted. I guessed it was the teacher in the pale yellow anorak. I slammed on the pedals. The bike lurched forward.

'Owww!' screamed Mandy as I bumped her to the ground and her leg caught the edge of the waste-paper bin.

'Hey, did you see that?' some boy yelled. 'Did you see what that kid just did to Mandy?'

'Get him!' someone shouted and the mob closed in. But as the first hands grabbed my arms and shoulders, something worse came winging through the air.

'DANIEL MILLER?!'

The power of the voice was awesome. I shook with terror. It was all I could do to balance the bike.

The female teacher in the yellow anorak was striding towards me, looking as if she'd cornered a rat. On her heels was another teacher. A man who shouldn't have been there at all. He walked up and whipped my sunglasses off. 'You're right, Jan. It *is* Daniel Miller,' he said. The female teacher nodded her head. Now I remembered where I'd seen her before. She had helped out once at a Willowbrook Open Day. Running a stall with her husband.

Mr Trewent.

CHAPTER 2

I was so frightened I could hardly breathe. As Mrs Trewent bent down to attend to Mandy (who was lying on the ground, blood running from her leg), Mr Trewent dropped a heavy hand on my shoulder. 'Right, bring your bike and follow me.'

He led me back across the road again and straight through the gates of Bushloe School. A crowd of inquisitive kids pressed forward.

'Who is he? What's going on?' they clamoured.

'He nobbled Mandy,' I heard someone say. 'Crocked her leg. He did it. Him.'

I felt like a dangerous criminal.

'There's nothing to see!' Mr Trewent bellowed,

dispersing the crowd with a wave of his hand. He flipped up the rear of a long, black car, shoved a few boxes of textbooks around, then lifted my bike and slid it inside. 'Get in, belt up and shut up,' he said. 'I'm locking you in – for your own safety. I'll be back when I've assessed the injury to the girl.' He pushed me inside and banged the door shut. The clunk of the locks was like an arrow in my chest.

When he returned, his face was grim.

'Is she all right, sir?' I asked him nervously.

He frowned and pulled his seatbelt on. 'No, Miller, she is not "all right". She has a badly gashed shin and will probably need stitches and a tetanus injection. My wife is taking her to Cottersthorpe hospital, which, I might say, is probably preferable to where you're going.'

'Sir, I've got to go home,' I wailed. Sitting in the car, I'd had time to think: if I wasn't at home when Mum came in . . .

'Don't be ridiculous, you're going to school. Where it's patently obvious you should have been this morning!'

'Sir, my appendix, sir,' I gabbled.

He glared at me hard. 'You astound me, Miller. Truancy, especially to this degree, is a very serious offence. Don't try to squirm out of it by making up any lame excuses. It won't win you any favours, believe me. I'm taking you to Mr Duberry's office. You can explain your conduct to him, in full.' And with that he fired the car to life, beeped at a crowd of bewildered kids and roared off along the Cottersthorpe Road.

Scott was the first to see me. I was hovering outside Mr Duberry's office when he burst down the corridor, whooping like an Indian.

'Newton, stop running and shut that noise!' a distant teacher commanded.

'Yessir,' said Scott, slowing down into a penguin walk. He waddled to my side. 'Ace. You're here. Trewent said in English you were—'

'Shut up-pp,' I hissed. 'He's in there, with the Blueberry.' I pointed to the half-closed door of the office. Mr Trewent was inside, giving his report of the Bushloe incident.

Scott clamped his mouth. 'So what you hanging round here for? Training starts at the next bell. Crozzy'll go mad if you're late.'

I lowered my head. 'I've got to see Duberry.'

'You? Why? What'd you do?'

'Went to Bushloe at dinner.'

'*What?*' He nearly jumped out of his shoes. 'What for? Does Crozzy know?'

'Does Crozzy know what?' We leaped to attention as Mr Crozier emerged from the staff-room

145

toilets, slicing a comb through his greased, black hair. 'What are you pair doing loitering round here?'

'Got to see Mr Duberry, sir.'

Mr Crozier examined me with pincer-sharp eyes. 'Have you been scrapping with Peters again?'

I shook my head.

'Well, what's going on?'

When I told him, he hit the roof. 'Bushloe? What the *hell* were you doing up there? I heard you were ill this morning.'

The office door slammed shut. Mr Crozier leaned forward and peeked through the glass. 'Is that Mr Trewent reporting you to the head?'

'Yes, sir,' I tremored. 'Mr Trewent caught me.'

'Sh—' Scott started, shutting his mouth before he could swear.

Mr Crozier muttered something under his breath, scratched his head and flicked a look at his watch. 'Newton, get to the gym and tell the others I've been delayed. I want them changed and on the pitch and doing light warm-ups by the time I get there. Is that understood?'

'Yessir,' said Scott, gulping quietly. 'See you later,' he muttered hopefully to me, and backed away looking pale and concerned.

'Right,' said Mr Crozier. 'Let's hear it from the

top. What *exactly* were you doing in Bushloe?'

I tried to tell him, but the words wouldn't come. I didn't know where to start. With the doctor, telling me to take the day off? Mum and the letter? The little devil on my shoulder? If I tried to explain about Billy and the video I knew he'd fly into a hopeless rage. In the end, none of it mattered. I spluttered out a string of meaningless words and Mr Crozier made up his own account. 'You've been checking out the opposition, haven't you? That's the truth of it, isn't it, Miller?'

I opened my mouth. He told me to shut it.

'You're a chuffing idiot,' he said. 'Now I'm going to have to go in there and somehow try to sort this out.'

At that moment, the office door rattled open. A stony-faced Mr Trewent stepped out. Mr Crozier acknowledged him tautly.

'Not training, Alun?' Mr Trewent said acidly. 'Thought you had a crucial match on Friday?' His cold gaze switched to me. 'Knock once and wait till the head calls you in.'

'Yes, sir,' I muttered. I knew the procedure.

But as I raised my fist, Mr Crozier tugged me back. '*I'd* like to speak to the headmaster first.'

He was talking to me, but eyeballing Trewent. I could tell by the brooding looks on their faces that they weren't exactly the best of pals. Mr Trewent produced a sickly smile. 'I hardly think it will do much good. You know the head doesn't tolerate *skiving*, Alun.' He glanced at me again. 'I'll expect you at break tomorrow, when you can catch up on the work you've missed.'

'Yes, sir,' I said, and he swept away.

'Right,' said Mr Crozier, cracking his knuckles. 'Stay there and leave this to me.' He knocked the glass once and barged into the office. The door slammed to, then opened a crack – enough to let me hear what was being said.

'Alun?' Mr Duberry's voice was even. 'Let me guess: you're here about young Miller?'

Mr Crozier faked a sigh. 'Just interrogated the berk, outside. These lads; I don't know what to make of them at times. One sniff of glory and they pop like a blooming champagne cork.'

'I don't follow you,' Mr Duberry said.

Mr Crozier perched on the desk. 'You know what it's like. We've both been there. Chance of a medal? Name on the Cup? They get so carried away with the prospect of silver their brains decide to take a holiday. Biking up to Bushloe to check the opposition. You have to admire their will to win.'

I heard the creak of the headmaster's chair. 'I don't call truancy "getting carried away", Alun. And using it as an excuse to spy on your opponents basically comes down to cheating, in my book.'

'Oh, come on-nn,' Mr Crozier objected. 'Laying it on a bit thick, that, isn't it? Cup fever – that's what I'd call it. You know Miller. He's a good, bright lad – the most promising young footballer this school's had in years. I'm sure this is just a silly aberration. Let me sort it out. A few stiff circuits of the gym. I guarantee it won't happen again.'

'Oh, you may be sure of that,' said Mr Duberry. 'And I might well have delegated punishment to you – if this was purely to do with football. I take it you don't know about the girl?'

'*Girl?*' Mr Crozier barked.

Just as a voice beside me said, 'Well. Look what's come rolling down the valley . . .' Marcia, in her netball kit, hair tied back in a scrunchie, looking gorgeous. She parted from her team and drifted towards me.

'*But that's ridiculous!*' Mr Crozier exploded, his voice so loud it rattled the glass.

'What's happening?' asked Marcia. She looked towards the office.

'*Punishment's one thing!*' Mr Crozier bellowed. '*But there's no need to make the whole team suffer!*'

'Is this about you?' Marcia looked me up and down.

I nodded, shaking a tear down my cheek.

'What have you done?' She reached out to touch me – just as the office door flew open.

Mr Crozier's anger flooded out like a wave. 'Well, I hope you're feeling pleased with your— Oh my giddy aunt! He's got *another* one now! Marcia, get to your lesson!'

Marcia stood her ground and let her fingers brush my wrist. 'Thank you for sending your mum with my essay. That was very thoughtful. You should have called me last night to cancel our date, but I'll forgive you as you haven't been *well*.' She glared at Mr Crozier and flounced away.

'How the heck did you pull that?' he muttered. 'No, don't tell me the sordid details. I'm sure I'll get to hear through the usual channels. Go on. Get your miserable face in there. You're an idiot, Miller. A nine-carat plonker. You've let the *whole school* down!' He thumped the wall hard and swept up the corridor.

Mr Duberry beckoned me into his office.

CHAPTER 3

'WELL, IT SERVES YOU DAMN WELL RIGHT!'

At home, the voices were different but the shouting went on.

'If I'd been Mr Duberry,' yelled Dad, flinging out his arms as he paced around the room, 'I'd have banned you for the rest of the season!'

I covered my eyes as the pain dug deep. Even now, an hour later, all I could remember of my 'talk' with Mr Duberry were those dreadful last words: 'In my experience, Miller, the only way to deal with a transgression of this kind is to give you a punishment befitting the crime. For that reason, I am suspending you from the match on Friday.

You will play no part in the game against Bushloe.'

'LOOK AT ME!' Dad roared again.

'Neville . . .' Mum said in a calming tone. Even she'd never seen Dad quite so furious. She was sitting on the sofa, Alice tucked up beside her.

'You know what irks me the most?' he said. He clenched his teeth and wagged a finger. 'The fact that you betrayed your mother's *trust*.'

I looked at Mum through tear-filled eyes. She hugged Alice to her and glanced at the jigsaw, still scattered all over the table. That was how I felt inside right now: shattered, in pieces, no-one wanting to put me back together. But Dad, in his own strange way, was trying.

'Why?' he begged, spreading his hands. The hurt in his voice spoke of years of loving care. 'Why did you do it? Why didn't you just *tell* us what the problem was? Instead of . . . deceiving your mother like that?'

'I did tell you!' I protested. 'And I didn't deceive Mum. Not really. It just . . . happened.'

I looked at Mum. She shook her head and sighed.

Dad glared at me again. 'You really expect us to believe this pain in the tummy nonsense?'

So was *that* what they thought? That I'd faked it just to get off school? 'It's true! It hurt when the doctor pressed me. He said I'd got a grumbling appendix.'

'Yes, well, it might be a fitting penance if you end up in hospital for your sins,' Dad growled. 'Which brings me to the other matter: this girl.'

'Girl?' muttered Alice.

'Hush,' said Mum.

Dad's mouth became a slash of anger. 'Amanda Woodruff. That's her name, isn't it? Two hours in Casualty at Cottersthorpe hospital.'

'He never hit her?' gasped Alice.

Mum shushed her again.

'It was an accident!' I cried. 'I didn't mean to hurt her!'

'Well, it's a damn good job you didn't,' Dad snapped. He was circling my chair now, closing like a hawk. 'According to Mrs Trewent, the girl is saying no harm was intended – which is rather fortunate for your mother and me. Any other day we might have found ourselves up in court, paying hundreds of pounds to remove the girl's scars. Do you understand what I'm saying, Daniel?'

I rocked in the chair. 'I'm sorry,' I bawled.

There was silence for a moment.

Alice broke it. 'He means it,' she said. 'Stop shouting at him now.'

I glanced at her through my parted hands. She was biting her hair and fighting back a tear. It was the first time I'd ever heard her take my side. She saw me peeking and stuck out her tongue, but for once I knew it was just an act. Deep down, somewhere, she really cared.

Dad fell into a chair and laced his fingers. His thumbs began to hammer out a nervous beat. 'Right,' he said, 'this is your punishment – the first part anyway. Go upstairs and make yourself presentable, then take ten pounds from your piggy bank. We're going to the florist's, via the paper shop.'

'Why?' Alice queried.

Dad threw her a glance. 'Your brother, at the tender age of thirteen, is about to find out how to treat a woman properly.'

Alice turned to Mum. 'He's got to buy you flowers?'

'Not me,' said Mum, with a shake of her head.

'Who, then?' I spluttered.

'Who do you *think*?' Dad said.

CHAPTER 4

I chose something called irises; white with reddish flecks; the closest I could get to Swansea City colours. A sign in the shop had said, SAY IT WITH FLOWERS. That was the plan: let the petals talk. Give flowers. Give chocolates. Mutter sorry. Go. But I was scared. Dead scared. Chewed up inside. Dad was going to drop me at the gate and wait. I had to face Mandy on my own, he'd said. Boy, was I going to look seriously uncool if she rolled up her sleeves, socked me in the mouth and told me to stuff my stupid presents. Worse, what if Adam came to the door? Mandy must have given him the letter by now. He was sure to want to know about the Willowbrook Duck. What if *he* stepped out and socked me in the mouth? I shuddered and the irises rustled in their wrapping. This had to be the worst day of my life, ever.

We pulled up outside a large new house with a straight green lawn and an apple tree in the garden. As the engine fluttered to a stop, Dad tried to give me some 'fatherly' advice. 'Think of it like a free kick,' he said.

I cast him a puzzled look.

'Just give it your best shot, OK?'

Yes, Dad. Mega-funny. Ha, ha, ha. Football was the *last* thing I wanted to think about as I made the long walk up that drive. Trembling, I rang the bell.

'I'll get it,' said a voice that could chisel granite.

I would have run had the door not opened so fast. A lad, about fifteen, came to the step. He had close-cropped hair, a ring in one ear and a T-shirt with HEADCASE written across it. 'Yeah?' he said.

'Is Mandy in, please?'

He parted the flowers, as if looking for the weed. 'You're him, aren't you? The kid that hurt my sister?'

I stepped back a pace. He stepped forward. Down the drive, I heard the sound of the car door opening. Dad, getting ready to come to my rescue. I was going to shove the flowers in the boy's face and run, when a stern voice shouted: 'Dean! Let him be.' Mandy dived out and smacked him on the arm. 'This is private,' she growled. 'Don't you dare touch him.'

Then a woman, smaller than the pair of them, appeared. 'Mandy? Dean? What's going on?'

'I've got a visitor, Mum.' Mandy gave me a frosty stare.

Mrs Woodruff glanced at the flowers and seemed to work everything out at once. 'Dean, take these to the bathroom, please.' She handed him a towel and a rubber duck. 'Tell Adam I'll be there in a minute.'

Duck. It was like some horrible sign. Weird, too. Adam Woodruff liked to bathe with a *rubber duck*? I wondered if his Bushloe team-mates knew. I looked warily at Dean. He snarled and dragged himself back into the house.

'Right,' said Mrs Woodruff, 'I'll leave you to it. I'm sure you two have plenty to discuss.' And whispering to Mandy to 'behave herself', she retreated too.

'Well?' said Mandy, tightening her lip.

I offered her the flowers. 'Got you these.'

She crossed her arms and stared at me hard.

'I brought some chocolates, too.'

At that, she stuck her nose in the air. 'Would you like to see my injury?' she said. Before I could answer she'd bent down and pulled up the leg of her jeans. Across the centre of her shin was a thin red line, neatly tied together with three black stitches. There were grazes and some bruising to the sides as well. It looked like a pretty painful gash. But the thing that surprised me most about her leg was not the damage I'd caused, but the shape of it: for a girl, she had a really muscular calf.

'Six days,' she said, leaving it showing, 'before I can have the stitches out. And I'm not allowed to do anything strenuous. So kicking you in the teeth is not an option – unfortunately.'

'Sorry,' I muttered, flinching a bit.

'My bum hurts, too,' she said with a snap. 'Two hours on a plastic seat in Casualty and then an injection – in case I get tetanus. Want to see that as well, do you?'

'No,' I gabbled as she started to turn. 'I believe you – honest.' I looked into her eyes. To my surprise (and shame), they were misting over.

'Why'd you do it?' she sniffed. 'Why didn't you just stop?'

I gave a feeble shrug. She must know by now I was bunking off school. I had to get away. Simple as that.

'Was it 'cos I snogged you in front of my mates?'

I thought about the kiss, then shook my head. 'No, that was . . . you know, all right.'

She scowled slightly and rubbed one eye. 'I showed Adam your letter.'

'Oh,' I said with a nervous twitch. I prayed he wouldn't come to the door right now.

'Mum posted it half an hour ago.'

'Thanks,' I said, then looked up, confused. What was she on about? *Posted* it? Where?

'It's only round the corner from here,' she said.

'What is?'

'Medlars Close,' she tutted. 'That's why I was trying to stop you at dinnertime. The letter you gave me was for someone called Arrowsmith.'

'*What?*' I thrust a hand into my pocket. To my horror, I pulled out the letter for Adam.

Mandy's face lit up. 'Hmph. Messed up, haven't you?' she said.

Not much! What a grade-one plonker.

'You gave me the wrong letter, didn't you?'

'Yes,' I said, whacking the real one against my thigh.

'OK. No worries. I'll take it,' she said, and leaned forward and nicked it from my hand.

'Hey! What you doing? Give that back!'

Quick as a flash, she turned and posted it through her letterbox, then quickly pulled the front door to. 'It's all right,' she said. 'I'll make sure Adam sees it.' There was a funny sort of satisfied chirp in her voice.

I held out my hand. 'Mandy, give it back. That letter, it doesn't really matter any more.'

'It mattered a lot this dinnertime,' she said.

'Mandy, *please*.'

She tilted her head. 'How do you know my brother, anyway?'

'I don't, OK? Someone told me about him.'

'What did they tell you?'

'That he was brilliant at football. Please, can I have that letter back?' It would only make things worse if Adam read it now. And if Mr Crozier found out what I'd done, I might never get to play for the school again.

But Mandy was having none of it. The more I squirmed, the more she revelled. 'Did you get into loads of trouble at school?'

'Yes,' I squeaked.

'Gonna tell me?'

'No.'

She cocked a petulant hip.

Oh well, what difference would it make if she knew? I was stuffed anyway. I might as well hang up my boots for good. 'I got suspended from the football team.'

She put her tongue in her cheek and gave a smug sort of grin. 'From Willowbrook's game against our school, on Friday?'

'Yes,' I growled. 'Don't you dare tell Adam.'

160

Clamping her lips, she paused to think. 'Bet you're dead good at footie, aren't you?'

I sighed and stubbed a toe.

'Top kid, yeah? Midfield supremo?'

Shrugging, I muttered, 'I've been watched by a scout.'

'Oh,' she said, and I thought I saw a mild look of envy in her face. But why would *she* be jealous of that? She noticed my puzzlement and snapped back, fast. 'OK,' she peeped. 'I won't tell Adam. Scout's honour, yeah? That's a joke. Do you get it?' She held out her hands. 'I'll have my flowers now, please.'

I gave a heavy-shouldered huff and thrust them at her. (What Dad must have thought of my technique with women!) 'Picked them 'cos you like Swansea,' I said.

For the first time, she smiled. Her cheeks caved in with two huge dimples. She wasn't bad looking really. Not pretty, like Marcia, but kind of . . . interesting.

She stroked a loose petal and swung her hips. 'Thanks. That's dead thoughtful – for a lad, I s'pose. But it doesn't excuse you for hurting my leg.'

'No,' I said.

'I'm really mad about that. You've caused masses of trouble at school, you know.'

161

'Yes,' I said, getting slightly tetchy. She didn't have to rub it in.

'You deserve your suspension. It's a red-card offence.'

'Yes,' I said, and pushed the chocolates at her in the hope she'd give her mouth something better to do.

'Ta. I'll give those to Mum.'

'But—?'

'I don't eat chocolate; bad for your physique – I mean figure,' she corrected. 'Bad for your figure.' She bopped me with the flowers to clear my frown. 'You gonna call me, then?'

'Call you? What for?'

'To see how I'm doing, stupid. If you're gonna bring flowers, I want to know you mean it. Cottersthorpe three six nine. We're not in the book, but a dozy gerbil could remember that number. You're not a gerbil, are you?'

I pulled a *fun-nee* face. Not in the book! No wonder my phone call plan had gone wrong. It had never even stood a fighting chance. 'Don't you hate me?' I asked.

Somewhere high above us a pigeon cooed.

'I ought to,' she said in a lofty tone. 'But things have sort of . . . evened out, I s'pose.'

Evened out? Before I could ask what she meant by that, she looked towards the car and quickly added, 'Your dad wants to go, I think. You could kiss me on the cheek, if you like, before you leave.' Her eyes flicked up like two blue magnets. She smiled shyly. Those dimples again.

I stood for a second, wondering what to do. The pigeon cooed. Another one joined it. Some strange force made me take a step forward. Mandy blinked once and turned her cheek. I was close enough to smell the shampoo in her hair when her mum shouted, 'Adam, don't go out in a towel!'

'Cripes!' went Mandy, turning so fast that I nearly fell flat on my nose on her step. 'Gotta go,' she gabbled, as the door began to open. She thumped it hard and a boy went, 'Ow!' 'Call me,' she said and squeezed through the crack.

Girls. They were weird. Totally *weird*.

CHAPTER 5

'Right,' said Mr Crozier, rolling a ball underneath his foot, 'this is where the blackboard theory ends and we have to start talking with our feet again.' He flipped the ball up and volleyed it into the back of the net. 'I've had a good look at the opposition and there's nothing whatsoever to be frightened of. They look a neat enough outfit, but as a team they're physically small.'

'Rubbish strip, too,' Ewan Thomas remarked.

We all peered down the Willowbrook pitch. In the goalmouth at the tennis court end, the tangerine-shirted Bushloe side were knocking a ball around, warming up.

'Which one's Woodruff?' Billy asked.

All eyes turned to me. I shoved my hands into the pockets of my parka. 'Don't know,' I mumbled, leaning back against a goalpost.

'Useless,' Hywel Dennis growled.

I couldn't have put it better myself.

Barring Mr Crozier, Hywel had been the first to discover what had happened in Mr Duberry's office. On his way to Games that afternoon, he'd dashed into the toilets and found me there, blubbing. 'Whassa matter?' he'd said, straddling a urinal.

'Been to Duberry,' I'd sniffed, washing my face.

For Hywel that was no big deal. He could pitch a tent outside the headmaster's office and no-one would question it; he was in there a lot. 'Whaddya do?'

When I told him, his face had turned ashen.

'But we'll lose!' he cried. 'If we haven't got you. What'd you go to *Bushloe* for?' He'd kicked a cubicle, making me cower. Hywel had been known to kick knees before.

'Dunno,' I wailed. And I'd bumped against a wall, sliding down into a pixie squat.

Hywel spat into a sink. 'What does Crozzy say?'

'He's mad.'

'No, *you're* mad,' said Hywel. And he'd snatched up his bag and hammered it against a towel dispenser. 'You're pathetic,' he'd roared and banged through the doors.

Two minutes later, he'd informed the whole team.

'His name's Adam,' Mr Crozier said, his dry voice dragging me back to the present. 'That's the sum total of Miller's little venture: if anyone wants to swap autographs, you'll be able to ask Mr Woodruff in person.'

More dark looks. Hywel swore.

'S'pose we'll see him soon enough,' said Scott. He folded his arms and stared Hywel down. Over the past two days Scott had been the only friend I'd had; the one member of the team I'd been able to talk to. He wasn't too thrilled about what I'd done, but at least he wasn't making me feel like a traitor. Then again, he didn't know the full story. When he asked about the phone call, I'd told him the truth: I couldn't find Woodruff's number in the book. But later, when we talked about the journey to Bushloe, I'd stuck to the 'checking out tactics' excuse. He didn't deserve a lie like that, but I was just too scared to tell about the letter.

In the centre of the pitch, a whistle went.

'Right,' said Mr Crozier. 'Here we go. Keep it tight. Give it everything you've got.'

'Sir,' the team chorused, melting away.

Only Billy lagged behind to tighten a lace.

'You've gone weird,' he said quietly, 'going up to Bushloe. We're still gonna win, though, even without you.'

'If you dive, it's not going to matter,' I said. 'We'll get disqualified. Just ask Scott.'

'Billy, move it,' Scott called, clapping loudly.

Billy tugged at his socks. 'We had a vote yesterday: I take free kicks and pens in this game.'

'You'll miss,' I said.

He wiped his nose on his sleeve. 'Loser,' he sneered and ran for the kick-off.

That hurt. That really hurt. I'd always given two hundred per cent and he knew it. But maybe he was right. Perhaps I was a loser. Whichever way you looked at it, I'd totally messed up. And not just with the team. Somewhere, right at the back of all this, I felt bad because I'd lost a good mate too. Me and Billy had been tighter than knotted string once. It made me wonder which was better: staying friends with someone or staying in the Cup?

I mooched towards a corner flag, head bent low, hands so deep inside my pockets they could have been searching for black holes in space. That was why I didn't see Mandy at first. I heard Mr Crozier greet the Bushloe teacher, looked along the touch-line – and there she was.

She had just jumped out of a bright blue car and

was hurrying towards my end of the pitch. She was wearing a pair of tracksuit bottoms and a padded lilac anorak, zipped right up to her bottom lip. Her hair, swept back beneath a wide Alice band, looked like the tail of a straw-coloured comet. 'Hmph, fancy meeting you here,' she said. 'Thanks for phoning me, *not*.'

'Sssh,' I muttered, flapping my hands, anxious not to draw Mr Crozier's attention.

'Charming,' she hooted. 'First you promise to ring, then you tell me to shut it.'

'I *did* ring. It was engaged, OK?'

'Sure,' she yawned. 'I've heard some excuses . . .'

'It's true. Anyway, I haven't been well.'

'You look all right to me. What's up with you, then?'

'Got a grumbling appendix.'

She cocked her head.

'It's *true*,' I said.

'OK. Prove it.'

'*What?*'

'Point where it hurts. Put your hand on it.'

'Mandy, get lost.'

She folded her arms.

I bounced a hand off my head in despair. What was it with girls? Why couldn't they just believe what we said? I took a quick look round to check no-one was watching, then touched the right-hand side of my groin.

'OK,' she peeped, and we started to walk. At last the conversation turned to something sensible. 'Rubbish pitch,' she muttered, eyeing the famous Willowbrook slope. 'Won't matter, though, we're still gonna stuff you.'

I decided not to rise to it and said something neutral: 'Have you come to watch Adam, then?' By now, the teams were changing ends. I scanned the boys heading for defensive positions. None of them looked particularly special.

'I've come to support the school,' she said, topping it with a tight-lipped smirk.

I looked at the Bushloe players again, carefully studying the team formation. They were settling into a flat back four. No sweeper. No Woodruff. 'Where is he?' I asked.

'At the dentist's,' she replied, hurring on her nails.

'DENTIST'S?' My shout nearly drowned the ref's whistle.

She pointed to a tooth at the back of her mouth. 'Mmm. Ish one, I dink. It *was* an emergency appointment, Mum said.'

Big deal! After all I'd been through! All the pain and the guilt and the tellings off. I get myself suspended from a crucial match, only to find that her brother has a flipping *dental appointment*?!

'You're lying,' I accused her.

'Oh, and look who's talking,' she said. She gave me a withering look, then sprinted down the touchline, cheering on her school.

In her wake came a sharp command. 'Miller! Get here, now!'

Mr Crozier was on the halfway line, giving me a frown that could blacken the sun. As Mandy shot past him, he eyed me with a mixture of awe and disbelief. 'Concentrate on the football, will you?'

'Sir,' I sighed, 'I've got something to tell you.'

'Talk about anything in a flipping skirt.'

'Sir, this is dead important.'

'*Get stuck in, Jonesy! Our ball, ref?!* Who is she anyway? Your latest conquest?' He glanced at Mandy, who was bawling encouragement across the pitch. 'Crikey, she's got a gob on her,' he muttered. 'You want to be careful, Miller – it's not wise having two birds in the nest.'

'Pardon?' I said.

'Come on-nn,' he said. 'Don't give me that. You and Miss Williams are the talk of the staff room.'

'*Pardon?*' I went again.

'*Tighter!*' he roared, as the ball skittered away

off Hywel's shin and Bushloe forced an early corner.

Mandy was immediately over the touchline. 'Jezza, come on, move up!' she waved. 'Just three at the back. Let the tall striker float!'

A spotty-faced boy went ambling forwards.

'Mr Crozier, Woodruff's at the dentist's,' I said.

But Mr Crozier's attention was focused on the corner – a good in-swinger to the six-yard box. Scott rose and headed it powerfully clear. But as Hywel tried to knock it out of harm's way, it ricocheted off a Bushloe player and came slithering back across the edge of the box.

'Hit it!' screamed Mandy as Jezza closed in.

I tensed my fists. It was a definite chance. One good strike and . . .

Wham! The ball sailed over the bar.

'Aww!' went Mandy, spinning round.

I breathed a sigh of relief. By rights, we should have been one–nil down. One minute gone and my heart was pounding. It slowed down a lot in the next thirty-nine.

That skyer turned out to be the closest shot on goal in the *entire* half. When the half-time whistle sounded there were groans of frustration all over the pitch. A string of our supporters gave a slow hand-clap. Billy tugged at his shirt in disgust.

Apart from one weak shot on goal, which had plopped straight into the keeper's arms, he'd barely been in the game at all. He hadn't had a single chance to dive.

Mr Crozier was not a happy bunny. '*That* was utterly pathetic,' he barked. 'I've seen my granny do better with an old balloon!'

Scott flopped out with his hands at his sides. 'We're missing Danny. We're dead in midfield.'

'Thanks,' moaned Hywel, scraping mud off his studs. Mr Crozier had moved Hywel into midfield to plug the gap I'd normally fill. He was plugging well enough, it had to be said. But accurate passing was not his strength; our front men were getting no sort of service.

'Which one's Woodruff?' Billy panted. 'None of them seem that smart to me.'

'They're not,' I interjected. 'Woodruff isn't playing.'

Mr Crozier showed me a cold dark eye. 'And how, pray, do you know *that*?'

'Sir, I did try to tell you, honest. That girl over there's his sister. She told me.'

'Her in the lilac with the hair?' said Scott.

'The one who keeps mouthing off?' said Ewan.

'Shut up,' said Mr Crozier. 'Are you sure about this, Miller?'

'Yes, sir. Woodruff's gone to the dentist.'

'Aw,' groaned Billy, and sagged to the ground.

Scott took a swig of water from a bottle. 'This is our best chance to beat them, then.' He looked at me, then at Mr Crozier.

Mr Crozier rubbed his chin. 'Right, change of tactics this half,' he said. 'We'll defend a little deeper and hit them on the break. Newton, as you're so disillusioned with your midfield men, try missing them out and hitting a few long ones over the top.'

'Route one,' said Hywel, elbowing Billy.

Straight into the duck-pond. Quack. Quack. Quack.

I spent the next forty minutes in silent prayer. But if anything, the second half was duller than the first. With five minutes to go the match was still goal-less. Billy, for all his devious skills, was having no luck with free kicks or penalties. Whenever the ball came anywhere near him the Bushloe defenders backed right off. Three times he hit the deck in the second half, each time failing to impress the referee. On the third occasion the referee actually stopped the game and trotted across to have words with Billy. I thought he was getting red-carded for sure. But the ref, a mild-mannered, friendly-faced bloke, merely enquired if Billy had a stone in his boot or something as he seemed to be losing his balance such a lot?

It was laughable.

In injury time, with the game going nowhere, Mandy drifted up the touchline towards me. 'This is rubbish. Worst game I've seen in ages. I hope you're better than the rest of your bunch.'

'Scott's playing well – our number five,' I said.

She nodded. 'He's put in a few good tackles. He should run with the ball more often, though, instead of hoofing it towards that duck—' She stopped, and threw me a sheepish glance.

'You read my letter.'

'Well, what did you expect?' she said tautly.

'It was private. You promised you'd show it to Adam.'

'I *did*. He thought your picture was nice.'

'Nice? What did he say about the message?'

She snorted at the sky and gripped her hair. 'Danny, haven't you twigged this yet?'

'Twigged what?' I said as a loud voice yelled: 'GO ON, SCOTT!'

Mandy and I looked up together. Scott was on a stumbling forward run, battling through a tired string of defenders. As he beat the last man I screamed at him to shoot. Another step and he'd lose control of the ball. With an effort, he scooped a shot towards goal. On target. Over the Bushloe keeper.

'No!' squealed Mandy.

My hands hit the air.

The ball came down – and hit the bar.

'Awwww!' went the crowd.

'FOLLOW IN!' yelled Mr Crozier.

Pheeeep! Too late. The game was over. Nil–nil draw. Replay at Bushloe.

'Aw,' went Mandy, patting her heart.

There were cries of 'unlucky' from both halves of the pitch.

Scott stood, head bent, in the penalty area. The Bushloe keeper patted his neck. Scott nodded, shook hands and picked up the ball. With one last twinge of disappointment, he wanged it into the darkening clouds.

'Mine,' said Mandy, and shoved me aside. The ball was dropping at a shallow angle. She skipped to her left, leaned back quickly and killed it stone-dead on her chest. It fell to her knee, then to her instep. She held it a second, then chipped a half-volley into my arms.

The ball struck me in the chest and bounced away .

'Nice control,' she said. 'I thought you were s'posed to be good at this game?'

My mouth had frozen open in shock.

'Shut your gob,' she giggled. 'You look like a doughnut.'

I tried. My jaw just wouldn't respond.

'Danny, you'll have sparrows nesting in a minute.'

I still couldn't close my mouth. I just stood there, thinking, 'If *she's* that good at ball control – what's her brother Adam like?'

'Oh, honestly.' She walked right up to me then, put a finger on my chin and tipped my mouth shut. 'Don't be mad at me,' she said, playing with a bobble on my parka hood. 'I was going to tell you eventually, honest. I was just upset about my leg and you were being completely thick. I was only, y'know, teasing you.'

'What about?' I spluttered.

Her mouth fell open in disbelief. 'Danny, you can't be that dumb, sure—?' Suddenly, her gaze switched over my shoulder. And now it was her turn to look a bit shocked.

'What's the matter?' I said, unaware that someone was coming up behind me. A delicate hand slipped round my arm.

'I'm ready,' said a voice. 'Bit early, sorry. How was the match? Did Willowbrook win?'

Mandy stumbled backwards. Her lower lip quivered.

'Mandy?' I said.

But her eyes were blazing. 'See you for the replay, *duckman*,' she sniffed, then turned and bolted across the car park.

'My God . . .' said a voice, before I could respond. Mr Crozier walked past with Scott and Billy. Their tongues were almost scraping the grass. 'How does he do it?' Mr Crozier muttered. 'Talk about flies round a honey pot.'

'Cheek,' said my date, tugging at the hem of her (very) short skirt. 'Well,' she asked, 'how do I look?'

'Great,' I gulped. Utterly stunning.

'Lead on, then,' she said. And we headed for the bus stop. Arm in arm. Marcia and me.

And I *still* hadn't twigged about Mandy Woodruff.

CHAPTER 6

Marcia was all Mum's work, of course.

After the dressing down from Dad, I'd spent some moments alone with Mum. She'd just sat there, twiddling her thumbs in her lap – waiting, I guessed, for some kind of sorry. Trouble was, I didn't know what to say, or what I could do to make things better. So in the end I'd just asked the question outright. She had thought about it for several seconds, then tilted her head towards the table. 'That would be a start,' she'd said.

She meant the jigsaw, of course; what I should have been doing instead of messing around in Bushloe. I'd nodded and bit my lip. If patching a group of zebras together was going to repair Mum's love for me, I'd stay up all night – all weekend, if I had to. But she had to want more than that.

'Yes,' she said, 'there is something else. You can honour our other arrangement. Marcia: you're inviting her for tea, remember?'

And somehow, I'd plucked up the courage and done it.

It was just like royalty had come. The table had been brought into the centre of the lounge, laid with a tablecloth and decorated with flowers. There were upturned glasses at every place. Bread rolls in a basket. Folded serviettes.

Mum and Dad were at their fawning worst. Once they'd recovered from the eye-popping shock of seeing their 'baby' with a stunner like Marcia, they were straight into squirm-producing mode.

'Hello, Marcia, I'm Danny's father.' Smile. Eye legs. Get clucked at by Mum.

'Go through, Marcia. Make yourself at home.' Eye hem-line, blouse buttons, bra-line, lipstick. Follow perfume trail like sniffer dog. Frown.

And then there was Alice, hovering in the background. Stiff. Tight-lipped. Hair in a *ribbon*. Looking like a fairy off a Christmas tree. Her big dark eyes followed Marcia's every movement.

'This is Alice, Daniel's sister,' said Mum. *Daniel?* Agh! Someone throw me to the lions, *perlease*. Thirty seconds in and I wanted to die.

Alice barged through the lounge door, holding it open.

'Thank you,' said Marcia, sweeping in.

Alice curtsied to her and stuck out her tongue.

'Pack it in,' mouthed Dad. 'Show Marcia to a seat.'

While Alice did as commanded, Dad leaned back and stuck a thumb in the air. 'Well done,' he whispered. 'She's quite a catch.'

'Neville!' Mum snapped.

Dad scuttled away like a scalded cat.

From nowhere, Mum seemed to magic up a comb. 'You might have made a bit of an effort,' she hissed, stropping it painfully through my hair.

'Mum, we're only having *tea*.'

'Tsk, you've so much to learn,' she said. She ran a wet finger across my eyebrows, turned me round and bustled me in.

We talked about school; we talked about netball; we talked about Marcia's drama group.

'Juliet?' said Mum, all coy smiles. 'Have you found yourself a nice Romeo, yet?'

Even Alice had to groan at that.

Marcia picked at her rocket salad and smiled as if she'd heard it all before.

When it came to pudding (cherry tart with cream), Mum bent down and almost roasted my ear. 'For goodness' sake, *say* something to the girl. Don't just sit there like a cardboard cut-out. What's got into you?'

Mandy Woodruff. That was what. I kept seeing her, stumbling away from Marcia. Eyes darting, lips quivering, hands grasping at nothing. I so much wanted to explain things to her, to tell her that it wasn't what she thought it was, to make her see that—

A nudge from Dad brought me back to the table. He was nodding at Marcia's glass. I vaguely remembered being asked to fill it. I lifted the jug of pineapple squash, but Marcia put her hand across her glass and said, 'No, thank you, Danny. I think I've had enough. Thank you for a lovely tea, Mrs Miller. The salad was super. I feel quite full.' She patted her tummy, making Alice glare; Marcia Williams was anything but fat. 'Danny, do you fancy going for a walk?'

I saw Dad wrestle a smile off his lips and do a little eyebrow traffic with Mum.

'Yes, that's a good idea,' said Mum. 'Why don't you take Marcia to the riverside, Danny?'

'Yeah, tie her to your bike and chuck her in,' Alice murmured.

Mum gave her a soft back hand. 'Dishwasher. Go and load it, please.'

Alice planted her feet and rose. 'You've got cream on your lip,' she said sourly to Marcia.

Marcia dabbed it with a serviette.

Alice stomped towards the kitchen with a pile of dishes.

'Don't think she likes me much,' said Marcia.

Dad smiled in apology. 'She's at that age.'

I took Marcia for a walk around the cricket pitch.

'This is nice,' she said, playing idly with a leaf. I could tell by the sound of her voice she didn't mean it; she was filling in the silences for something to do. 'Do you play cricket?'

I shook my head. 'Dad does.'

She smiled and said, 'He's funny, your dad. And your sister. Eyeing me all through tea, she was.'

'She's a pain,' I said, looking away.

'Is that what you think about all girls, then?' She grabbed me by the arm and tugged me down onto a bench. 'Let's sit here and have a cosy chat, shall we? I'm cold. You can put your arm round me if you like.'

Gulping, I closed my fingers around her. I felt

the strap of her bra through her wafer-thin top and shifted my grip a little further down her arm.

Leaning closer, she said, 'You still haven't told me why you were outside Duberry's office.'

I shrugged and her hair fell against my neck. It was soft and fresh and smelled like honey. 'Doesn't matter,' I mumbled. 'It's nothing major.'

'Fibber,' she said. 'You're all glum inside. You don't have to be a mind-reader – or a girl – to know that. It's got something to do with the game today, hasn't it? Why weren't you playing? Tell me, come on.'

She squeezed my side, so I poured it out. About Billy and Mandy, the letter, Mum and Dad. The further I went, the easier it became. Just like a long confession. She didn't ask questions or interrupt, just gave the odd nod or an 'hmm' now and then.

At the end she said, 'He's a prat, Billy Peters – but so are you for bunking off school. Did you really have a grumbling appendix?'

Shrugged again. 'That's what the doctor said. Can I move now, please? I think my fingers have gone to sleep.'

She sighed gently and craned me free. 'What about the replay? Can you play in that?'

I told her I hadn't thought about it.

'Tch,' she went. 'Don't be such a lettuce. Go and see Mr Crozier, first thing on Monday. Fight for your place. That's what I'd do. And forget about that stupid duck.' She crossed her legs and brushed a hand across her skirt. Her long, slim thighs, glossy brown in tights, rustled with static as she tugged her hem. 'There,' she said. 'Football sorted. Now, let's do the important stuff.'

I looked at her blankly.

'Mandy,' she said. 'Don't try to look surprised. You were moping about her *all* through tea.'

Speechless, I stared at the ground. My cheeks began to glow like a pair of cricket balls.

'It's a girl thing,' she said, 'in case you're wondering. We can always tell. It's called feminine intuition.' She pulled a woollen hat from her tiny denim bag and covered her hair to the level of her ears. Some girls would have worn it like an old tea cosy; it made Marcia look like a magazine model. 'Want to know what else?'

'What?' I muttered.

'She's got it pretty bad for you. Fancies the pants off you, in fact.'

'But she's mad at me,' I said.

Marcia patted my hand. 'No. Not really – but she isn't half spitting feathers about me. Did you like it?'

'What?'

'Danny, don't act.'

'What?' I repeated.

She prompted me again with her perfect lashes.

'*What?*' I said again and gazed across the pitch. A lone seagull was pacing the worn stretch of green. It looked about as lost as I did.

'Did you like it when she *snogged* you, of course?'

Oh that. I flicked a dead leaf onto the path. 'She was showing off in front of her mates, that's all.'

Marcia cocked her head. She turned sideways and gently parted my fringe. 'Hmm, but that's not what I asked you, is it?' She circled a finger over my knee. I looked straight ahead and counted gulls. My other knee sprang an uncontrollable jerk.

'Trouble is,' she whispered, her breath on my face, 'you've nothing to compare it with, I s'pose.' And before I had a chance to speak another word, she had bent round and put her mouth against mine, moving her lips so gently, so warmly, I felt sure I would melt through the slats of the bench.

It lasted just a couple of seconds. Then she pulled back again, clicking her tongue. 'So, what are you going to do about her, then?'

'Who?' I said.

She let her eyes roll.

About Mandy? Nothing. I told her so.

'Wrong,' she said, as if banging a gong. 'You should start with a phone call. *I'd* want a call at the very least. I wouldn't have you back – not straight away, like. But it would be a start. I'd be pleased you were making an effort.'

Was I hearing this right? 'You want me to *ring* her?'

'No,' Marcia tutted, sagging her arms. 'I want you to juggle carrots for her. Honestly – lads. I think you have "dumb" written into your genes.'

Dumb? I was mega-confused. 'But won't that be . . . y'know, two-timing?' She *had* just snogged me, after all.

Swinging her foot in a little arc, she said, 'You might as well know that I'm not going out with you.'

'But why did you—?'

She reached over and pressed a finger to my lips. 'Sssh, it was just a need-to-know thing. You're dead cute, Danny, and you look much older than you really are. Don't be upset. I'm not chucking you, OK? Tea with Mum and Dad doesn't count as going out. And I do sort of fancy you . . . in a toy-boy way; but . . . you're just not ready for me yet. *She*, on the other hand, is mad for you. You should go for her. It'll be good experience. I'll help you. I'll tell you what to say to make her swoon. There will be a price, of course.'

I narrowed my gaze and looked at her.

'Eddie Newton's mobile number,' she said.

186

'Scott's brother? He's in Year Ten.'

She laid a hand across her chest and fluttered her lashes. 'Shock, horror. What a tart I am.'

'But—?'

'Oh, come here,' she said with a laugh. She pulled me forward and snogged me again. 'There. That's on account. I might be back for the interest one day. Then you should really start to worry. For now, let's just be friends, OK? You know you like Mandy. So go for it. Right?'

'Are you sure?' I asked. She'd been steaming on the pitch.

Marcia took my hand and pressed it to my heart. 'Trust me. It's a girl thing. Just ring her, you dork.'

CHAPTER 7

Later that night, I tried. Mrs Woodruff picked up the phone. 'Hello, Bushloe three six nine?'

'Is Mandy in, please?'

'Is that Danny? Danny Miller?'

'Yes.'

'Just a minute.' She rested the phone. I heard a muffled exchange of female voices, then Mrs Woodruff was back. 'I'm sorry, Danny. I'm afraid that Mandy is . . . washing her hair.'

'Oh,' I said. 'Do you know how long she'll be?'

Mrs Woodruff coughed politely. 'Mandy's hair can take a long time to dry.'

'Shall I ring back in half an hour, then?'

'I'm afraid it takes a bit longer than that. Several days, on average.'

'*Days?*' I exclaimed. I knew that Mandy had a lot of hair, but . . .

Mrs Woodruff lowered her voice. 'Danny, listen. A word of advice: when a girl tells a boy she's "washing her hair", it means she's upset and doesn't want to talk – unless she's washing her hair, of course. Do you understand?'

'I'm not sure,' I muttered.

'You will,' she said. 'It's all a part of growing up.'

'Oh,' I said, furrowing my brow. I felt like a dog being patted on the head.

'Is there a message I could give to Mandy, once her hair's . . . you know, dried out?'

I opened a piece of paper in my hand. Marcia had given me some lines to say, coached me in the park with some lovey-dovey stuff. But I decided I would try to keep it simple, stick as close to the truth as possible. 'Tell her . . . it wasn't what she thought it was.'

Mrs Woodruff immediately groaned. 'Oh dear, you mean there's another girl involved?'

I scratched my head. How did *she* guess that?

'All right, I'll tell her, though I'm not really sure it will do much good. If you want my advice I'd try again tomorrow, sometime after the football results. She'll be in a good mood if Swansea have won. Football, that's the key to her heart. Take care now. Goodbye.'

Swansea lost. So I rang again on Sunday. On the first occasion, the phone was engaged; the second time she'd gone out somewhere with Donna; the third time Mandy herself picked up.

'Hi. It's Danny.'

Silence.

Fidget.

Football, key to her heart. Think footie. 'Bad news that Swansea got trashed yesterday.'

I thought I heard an inward rush of breath.

'They could still make the play-offs this season, though.'

The breath became a snort. And finally, she spoke, 'At the third stroke, it will be four thirty three precisely. Bip, bip, bip . . .'

'Look, it wasn't what you thought, OK?'

'Bip, bip . . .'

'You've got really nice eyes; they sort of sparkle when you laugh.'

'At the third stroke, it will be . . .'

'Mandy, stop goofing about, will you?'

'Bip, bip . . .'

'She was just my cousin from Cornwall,' I tried.

'Liar!' she snapped. 'Her name's Marcia

Williams, she lives in Cottersthorpe and every-thing in trousers fancies her.' There was a whoosh of air as the phone went down. Another whoosh as it came back up. 'And don't bring me any more flowers – unless you're planning to use them on your grave! Oh, and we're gonna stuff you out of sight on Tuesday. And my eyes don't sparkle, they *glow*, OK?!'

I reported this to Marcia at school on Monday. 'Ouch,' she said. 'Recognized in Cottersthorpe.' She winced and gave a sheepish grin. 'Better not ring her again this week. She'll have gone into nuclear meltdown now.'

'She hates me,' I said.

Marcia shook her head. She put a grip between her teeth and gathered her hair. 'Don't be dumb. She's just being prickly, that's all. She thinks she had something going with you and now you're just two-timing her.'

'But that's stupid,' I groaned, toe-poking a locker. 'I never said I'd go out with her.'

'That doesn't matter. She's hot for you.' She hoisted up her bag. 'Has she seen you in your shorts?'

A group of passing girls overheard that and giggled.

'Bum,' said Marcia, having a quick peek. 'It's

vital. Trust me. You look quite pert in your kit. Did you get me Eddie Newton's number yet?'

'Marcia. Will you please shut up about bums? I'm suspended, remember? I can't—'

'Miller?!'

Oh great, just what I needed then, Mr Crozier sticking his big nose in. 'Tuck your shirt in, boy. It's a uniform, not a pair of pyjamas.'

'Yes, sir,' I moaned, tucking in.

'The head wants to see you.'

'Sir? What about?'

Mr Crozier tapped his chin. 'Now, let me think, he did say something in the staff room this morning about asking you to run the school for a week. HOW SHOULD I KNOW WHAT HE WANTS? JUST MOVE YOURSELF!'

I glanced at Marcia, who was already backing off down the corridor. 'Bum,' she mouthed and blew me a kiss.

'Lord, save us,' Mr Crozier groaned.

'Sir?' I queried.

'HEAD!' he barked, and practically blew me into the office.

Mr Duberry invited me to stand by his desk. 'This football match against Bushloe,' he said, sifting through some papers in a filing cabinet. 'Given me a bit of a problem, hasn't it?'

'Don't know, sir,' I said, shuffling my feet.

'A nil–all draw. That's a replay, isn't it?'

'Tomorrow,' I said. My heart sank at the thought of another missed game.

He closed the cabinet and settled in his chair. 'Strictly by the book, you've got me in a corner, given me a moral dilemma of sorts. I told you, did I not, that you couldn't take part in the match last Friday?'

'Yes, sir,' I nodded, wishing he'd hurry up and get to the point. I was late for English. Trewent would go spare.

'Well, Friday has come and gone,' he said, 'but the game is still undecided, of course.' He took a gold-rimmed fountain pen from his pocket, unscrewed it and scratched a few words in his diary. 'So, the question is: do I let you take part in the replay or not?'

I sucked in sharply.

'What would you do in my position, hmmm?'

'Don't know, sir,' I said, swallowing hard. I had to grip my jacket to stop my hands trembling. Was he going to let me off or what?

He put the pen down and brought his hands together. 'What you did last week was foolish and irresponsible. A serious misdemeanour that could have seen you suspended not only from the team but also from the school. Indeed, had your attendance record been anything other than exemplary I might well have been forced to take such action, which would have made an unpleasant stain on your report and been of considerable embarrassment to your parents.'

'Yes, sir,' I muttered, looking at the floor. He tapped his left foot several times. I could see myself reflected in the shiny, bright toe.

'I won't tolerate renegade behaviour, Daniel. This is a school, not a rabbit run. However, I am prepared to accept that errors of judgement can be made. And while I remain dubious about Mr Crozier's slightly blinkered assessment that you were suffering from "Cup Fever", I can understand what this game must mean to you.' He paused and leaned back in his chair. 'What lessons have you learned from this incident, hmmm?'

I chewed my lip and mumbled back, 'It's not right to bunk off from school, sir. It causes loads of trouble with your teachers, and your mates. My mum and dad were dead upset too. It was stupid. I won't do it again. Ever.'

'Good,' he said. 'That is precisely what I wanted to hear.' He rocked forward in his chair again. 'You may tell Mr Crozier your suspension is lifted. I'm sure he'll be quite relieved.'

'Yes, sir. Thanks.' Never mind Crozzy. I wanted

to scream it out of the window. *I can play against Bushloe High!*

'Go on, clear off,' Mr Duberry added kindly. 'In case you haven't noticed, I've a school to run.'

'Yes, sir! Sorry, sir!' I whisked away.

'Oh, and Daniel.'

'Sir?'

'Saw a nice move on *Football Italia*. Del Piero free kick. Waited for the wall to jump then hammered it low, underneath their feet. Nearly scored, too. Clipped a post. Unlucky.' He caught my eye. 'Behave yourself, all right?'

'Yes, sir,' I said.

And he pointed to the door.

CHAPTER
8

'Anyone bring a map?' Mr Crozier grumbled as we trekked across the Bushloe playing fields searching for their team and their football pitch. 'How to beat the opposition: take them on a mile hike just before the kick-off. Any sign of a goal-post, Dennis?'

'There,' replied Hywel, who was some way ahead. He pointed past a row of poplar trees. A spray of tangerine shirts appeared.

'Hurrah,' said Mr Crozier and punted a ball into the empty goalmouth. Hywel went haring after it, giving us one of his running commentaries. *'And it's Dennis. He beats one man, he beats two, he beats the entire Bushloe defence and . . .'* he whacked the ball into the open net *'. . . scores!'* He dropped to his knees with his fists raised skyward. The Bushloe players turned our way. And that was the moment the game took on a whole new meaning.

'Hey,' said Ewan, 'it's that loud-mouthed girl.'

I heard the gasps of surprise but didn't understand them right away. My gaze had switched to the gaggle of supporters along the touchline. I was looking for something lilac with hair when Scott said, 'Look at her. She's giving us the eye.'

And finally I saw what everyone did.

She was on the D of the penalty area, kitted out in the Bushloe orange. She had her hands on her hips and her nose in the air, rolling a ball gently under her foot.

'Do you think she's their mascot or something?' said Ryan.

Mandy answered in spectacular fashion. She flicked the ball up, hit it high into the air, turned as it dropped and volleyed it towards the Bushloe goal. It clattered the underside of the bar, flashed to the ground and rebounded into the roof of the net.

Every drop of blood in my body *froze*.

'Who *is* that girl?' Mr Crozier said, frowning.

'Woodruff . . .' I muttered. And at last, I twigged.

A. Woodruff. *A*-manda Woodruff. *Adam* wasn't the Bushloe superstar. *She* was.

'Woodruff?' said Billy.

'He's a girl,' I spluttered. 'I mean . . . *she's* a girl. His name's Amanda. I mean . . . oh, it doesn't matter.'

But it did matter. It mattered a lot. Suddenly, everything began to make sense: the phone call from *her* when I'd rung her Uncle Colin; the anger of her mates when they knew I'd crocked her; her rush to shut the door when I'd taken her the flowers; those muscular legs; her ball control. Talk about sick as a parrot; thicker than a milk shake, that's what I was. All this time I'd been trying to warn Adam, never once suspecting that Mandy was the one. The best of it was she must have guessed what I was up to and still let me think her brother was the star. Teasing, she'd called it. A girly joke. I kicked a loose piece of turf into touch. If that volley was anything to go by she wasn't in the mood for joking now. She had scores to settle, on *and* off the pitch. This was a grudge match, no doubt about it. We might just as well have painted the touchlines red.

'Let me get this straight,' Mr Crozier broke in. 'Are you trying to tell me . . . Cinderella there is the Bushloe sweeper?'

'Yes,' I said. 'She didn't play last time because . . . she was injured.'

Billy threw up his hands. 'But I thought she – I mean he – was at the dentist's? Sir, I'm confused.'

'So am I,' said Scott, trying to unlock me with a penetrating stare. He knew I knew more than I was really letting on.

'She fooled us,' I said, hoping Scott would understand.

Ewan Thomas saved me from having to say more. 'Sir?' he asked. 'How can Bushloe play a girl? No-one else plays girls. Isn't there a law?'

Mr Crozier did not respond directly. He was channelling his gaze into the Bushloe half and muttering something under his breath. 'Ye-ss. Very funny, Mr Trewent. Very funny.'

'Trewent?' queried Billy. 'What's he got to do with it?'

'His wife teaches here. He must have known,' said Scott.

'You mean Trewent's the "mole"?' Hywel looked up, surprised.

'Rat, more like,' Scott went on plainly. 'If he'd told us straight who Woodruff was . . .' His words tailed off, but I knew what he was thinking. If Trewent had bothered to tip us off properly, I might have thought twice about contacting . . . her.

Trewent. He'd been laughing at us. Playing games. Playing a private teacher's joke. I wished I could beam him down to Bushloe, then. I was sure Mr Crozier would chin him, just for fun.

From the centre of the field came the peep of a whistle.

'Yes, well,' said Mr Crozier, cracking his knuckles. 'Boy, girl or alien, it's too late now. You all know your jobs. Let's get the game won.' And with one last look at the girl in orange, he sloped off the pitch and left us to it.

One thing was certain, right from the kick-off: Bushloe *with* Mandy was a whole different ball game from Bushloe without her. She was the glue that bonded them together. They played for her. They ran. They listened when she shouted. She wore the captain's armband. They obeyed her command.

On the field, she was tireless. When the ball ran loose, she was there to cover. If the play became tight, she would tidy up the mess. She sprayed passes around like a sprinkler system. A sweet chip here. A tap-back there. She could whip in a deadly, curling cross or split an indecisive back four open with a dangerous, daisy-cutting, neatly-weighted through-ball. Her boots *spoke*. She was as gifted as any boy I'd ever seen. In a word: awesome.

In possession, and running, she seemed unstoppable. As early as the fourth minute she pounced on a hesitant pass from Hywel and drove forward on a direct line for goal. Spurred on by her team-mates and shouts from the touchline, she brushed two challenges aside with ease and powered her way into the danger zone. Mud flew off her heels. Hair streamed out like a comet's tail behind her. Scott forced her wide, but not wide enough. She had the momentum and the pace to go past him. He stretched a leg and clipped her. She stumbled, lurched. I saw Ewan, in goal, freeze in horror. If she hit the deck, it was a penalty for sure. But she didn't hit the deck. She hit the target instead. She recovered her balance and let fly with a shot that almost knee-capped Ewan before rippling his net. Her team, like coats on a party bed, buried her. Eleven gobsmacked Willowbrook players gaped at each other, wondering what to do. We had seen the Bushloe superstar in action.

And we had no answer to her.

By half-time we were three–nil down. It should have been nine. Maybe nineteen. The crossbar, the posts, some heroics from Ewan, two breathtaking goal-line clearances from Scott kept the distance between us respectable. But we were on the back foot throughout the whole half. We defended so deep we were almost in trenches. Our six-yard box was like a motorcycle dirt track. Even Billy Peters, the celebrated goal-hanger, was forced to join the defensive blockade. Attack upon attack; the pressure unending. We had never faced an onslaught like it before.

Mr Crozier laid into us, hard. He threw orange segments at us as he dished out the caustic. 'That has got to rank as one of the worst displays of football I've ever seen. It's a shambles. A complete and utter ruin. You're supposed to be a team, playing for one another, not floating around like dandelion seeds. If it wasn't for this lad, and this lad here (he dropped a hand on Ewan's shoulder, another on Scott's), we might as well have packed up and made our way home! As for your movement off the ball, I've seen my goldfish look more organized. And what the *hell's* got into you?' He stabbed a finger at my chest. 'My sofa could outrun you today. You're shuffling around like a concussed rabbit. Are you carrying an injury or something?'

I shook my head and mumbled, 'No.' I hadn't thought about my groin. I hadn't thought about anything. I just couldn't seem to get into the game. Mandy's game. I was dazzled. We all were.

'It's that girl,' moaned Hywel (and several lads nodded). 'She's everywhere, sir. She's like a flipping whirlwind.'

'I still say she shouldn't be playing,' muttered Ewan.

'Oh, please, spin another record,' said Crozzy. 'I don't give a fig if she's eligible or not. The fact is she's there and making monkeys out of all of you. We've got to change our tactics and phase her out.'

Billy spat some orange peel over his shoulder. 'How?' he sniffed.

'Well, you could try *tackling* her for a start,' said Crozzy. 'What are you scared of? That she'll run and fetch her dad? For crying out loud, stop thinking of her as a girl, a *novelty* item, and treat her for what she really is.'

'An opponent,' said Scott, with his head bowed low.

'Exactly,' said Crozzy, 'and a good one at that. Right, listen up. This is the plan. Dennis, you're the cock of this year group, aren't you?'

'Natch,' he said, chewing.

'Good. Hear this. If you want to retain that dubious status I suggest you get your act together and deal with this girl. I want you to mark her out of the game. Stick to her tighter than the gum on your desk. First time she sees the ball, give her some clog. I don't mean damage her, just let her know you're there. Scott, you're doing famously at the back, but push up whenever you can, OK? The last thing madam will expect to see

203

now is you taking the game to them from deep. Strikers, you can't expect service if you keep your gobs zipped. Nor do you need a passport to enter the opposition's half. Let's see more aggression, more hunger, shall we? Full-backs, find those overlap positions. And Miller, get a grip and start spreading the play. I think they might be vulner-able to crosses. If we can plant a couple on Peters's head we'll have a realistic chance of opening them up. I know we'll be stretched if they hit us on the break, but what have we got to lose?'

In the background, the referee called, 'One minute.'

Mr Crozier crouched among us. 'Come on, lads, we can turn this round. If we get one back in the first few minutes, I reckon they'll go to pieces. Without the dancing queen, this lot are nothing. They're average; she's brilliant. But even the best players crack under pressure. Let's show them what we're capable of, eh?'

'Yes, sir,' we muttered, and rose to our feet.

On the way to our positions, Scott pegged me a moment. 'Have you seen him?' he asked. 'The bloke on the touchline?' He nodded towards a middle-aged man, dressed in grey trousers and a sheepskin jacket. 'He's been making notes, in a small red book.'

'The scout?' I gasped.

Scott gave a half-shrug. 'Don't care if he is or he isn't a scout. Don't care about the duck . . . or you and her.' He paused and glanced down the pitch at Mandy. 'I know there's something you haven't told me. She's got something on you. That's why you're not playing. You can spill if you want to, after the game. I'll still be your mate, whatever happens.' He showed me five. 'Just play a bit, yeah?'

In the distance Mandy bellowed, 'Come on, Bushloe. Keep it tight.'

I looked at Scott and slapped his palm.

Play a bit. Yeah.

It was time to make a comeback.

CHAPTER
9

From the whistle, they rolled the ball straight to her feet. Whoever said she was a sweeper had no grip on football. She was playing my role, centre midfield. Shadowing me, for all I knew. But in this half she had a shadow of her own. As she trapped the ball and started looking round for an option, Hywel homed in like a laser-guided missile. She saw him coming and dragged the ball back. Hywel slid past and collided with another Bushloe player. The clash drew Mandy's concentration for a second – and in that moment, I tackled her. The ball became the meat in a soft leather sandwich. We scrabbled. She fought. But her balance had gone. As she toppled, I flicked the ball off her toe.

'Hey, ref!' she protested.

'Fair challenge,' he called.

'Well won!' yelled Mr Crozier. 'That's more like it.'

'Danny, wide!' cried Scott, coming up in support. I threaded a dream of a pass to his feet. The Bushloe defence dissolved like candy floss. Scott was away, down the right channel.

We surged towards the Bushloe goal, Billy chirping like a parrot for a cross. Scott looked up and looped one in. The Bushloe keeper punched it clear. Who was there to meet it? Mandy Woodruff.

In a flash, Hywel came snapping at her heels. With two neat touches she skipped away again, spitting words of anger as he tried to grab her shirt. *Wham!* I clattered her again, from the side. She flashed an arm across my chest, trying to shield possession. As I pressed her, her wrist knocked up against my chin. *Pheep!* The referee signalled a foul.

Mandy twirled on her heels and stamped down hard. 'No way!' she complained. 'He was barging me, ref!'

'I'll be the judge of that,' he said. 'Watch your lip, number four.'

'Yeah, don't get your knickers in a twist,'

muttered Hywel, shoving Mandy roughly aside as he placed the ball down, ten yards inside the Bushloe half.

'Do your worst, dog breath. I've heard them all,' she sneered. She backed away mouthing, 'Watch it, Miller.' It was the first time in the game we'd looked at one another. It wasn't a pretty exchange.

I ignored her. At least I pretended to. Deep down I *still* had the urge to run up and tell her that me and Marcia weren't an item. Why couldn't she accept it? Why wouldn't she believe me? I drove my frustration into the ball, swinging in a cross that was way too high. The heads went up, but none made contact. The ball ran away for a Bushloe goal kick.

'Concentrate,' Mr Crozier clapped.

I glanced at the forwards, grimacing a 'Sorry'. As the teams readjusted, Mandy came close. 'Pity your duck can't fly,' she poked.

'At the third stroke . . .' I said.

'Fun-nee,' she hissed, putting herself in front of me as the goal kick soared into the centre circle. We jostled. She bumped me and leaned right back. Under any other circumstance I might have been happy to be shouldering her weight with my face full of frizzy, 'pineapple' hair. But when her hands came round and touched my thighs I thought she was going for the front of my shorts. I didn't need any video nasties to know what a move like *that* might mean. So I backed off fast to protect myself – and over she went again.

Once more the referee waved play on, impressed, perhaps, that my arms were free and my eye had never left the flight of the ball. I chested it down and ran away, clear.

Up front, Billy was my only option. He had his back to the goal, one defender behind him. I knocked it to his feet and went for the lay-off. Billy, as usual, stopped the ball dead. He shielded possession, inviting a challenge. A ponytailed stick of a lad closed in. From behind me Mandy shouted, 'Jezza, stand off him.'

Too late. Billy was starting to turn.

It was smart the way he fell. You had to give him that. He made it look ugly, without the drama. The ball bobbled free. Someone booted it clear. A blast of the whistle soon brought the play back. Free kick to us on the edge of the area. Mandy led the angry band of dissent. 'Wake up, ref. He *played* for that.'

The referee beckoned Mandy to him. 'I'm not going to tell you again, number four. Take a moment to think, OK? You're three goals up in a cup tie and coasting. But if you carry on like this, you're very soon going to be one player short. Do I make myself clear?'

Mandy did a hacked-off, pastille-chewing act and turned away, muttering under her breath.

'Direct,' said the ref. 'Wait for my whistle.'

'Wall, Mand. Come on.' The team urged her back.

Still chuntering, she organized a five-man wall, then joined the jam of players buzzing round the far post.

'Gonna bend one?' whispered Hywel.

I shook my head. This team knew us. Somehow, someway, they'd done their homework. I felt sure they knew to expect a curler. So I tried something different. A Duberry special. On the run-up I hesitated half a second, let the wall jump and kept my shot low. The ball skittered and zinged across the hips of mud and – *whup!* thudded off the base of a post, rebounding into the scrimmaging ruck. Feet swept under it. Shins gave it spin. There were two half-contacts. Cries of 'Clear!' A block. A deflection. Shouts of desperation. Then the zip and rustle of nylon netting, followed by a squeal of uncut joy. We had scored. No protests. No infringements. The referee was signing to the centre spot. I clenched my teeth and balled my fists. In the goalmouth, the happy acrobatics started. At the base of the pyramid of bodies was Billy.

From that moment on there was no stopping us. We pounded Bushloe as they had pounded us.

Now it was *their* shirts, *their* goalposts, *their* thighs carrying the smudges of a wet and muddy football. Mandy, for all her driving encouragement, could not restore their confidence, nor contain the storm. Twenty minutes after Billy's speculative punt, he scored again. And this time, Mandy was the fly in his trap. She had dropped back into a sweeper position, trying to shore up an anxious defence. Whenever Billy saw the ball she was there to ghost him, timing her tackles to absolute perfection, never once giving him the chance to dive. But in the end, he undid her with the meanest trick of all.

It started with a cross from Ryan Jones, a swirling effort off the inside of his boot, delivered, at pace, to the near-post zone. Mandy whipped across the stud-pocked turf. She looked set to make a comfortable interception, when, from among the clutch of shirts, a shout went up: 'Leave it, Mand.' Mandy hesitated, lifted her foot. The ball ran free across the face of the goal. The keeper, frozen with confusion, jerked. Billy Peters saw a stride and whacked the ball past him. His shot hit the bottom of the net so hard it cracked a wooden peg and sent a splinter into orbit. The referee pointed to the centre spot.

Goal.

The arguments broke out right away. Four

Bushloe players surrounded the ref, all claiming Billy had made a false call. While they put their case for 'unsporting conduct', the duck grew wings and swooped out of the area. Mandy took off in hot pursuit. Haring round in front of him, she squared up and cut his celebrations dead. 'You pig. You miserable, cheating *pig.*'

'Stuff off,' he sneered, and tried to brush past.

She slapped her hands on his chest and pushed him back.

Billy, not thinking, mirrored the act. There was a gasp. I heard someone say, 'Flipping heck, he's groped her.' Mandy looked down at her front. Billy's paw marks were spread right over her . . . bits.

The referee moved at the speed of light. 'That's enough. Break it up, you pair. Come on.' He drove his steepled fingers between them and forced them apart by widening his hands.

'Perv!' yelled Mandy.

'You started it,' said Billy, his cheeks glowing hotter than a couple of lightbulbs.

'Let's stick to the football, shall we?' said the ref.

Mandy almost poked Billy in the eye. 'He put me off deliberately. Book him, ref.'

'I can only give what I see,' he said.

'Look harder, then,' she barked.

And that, we all knew, was a step too far.

The referee reached for his bright-yellow card.

'You're *joking*?' she gasped.

'Do I look like a clown?' the referee said. He wrote down her name and number.

She turned away, flinging her arms to the sky. Or was it the sky? Was she appealing to the man on the touchline? The scout. The mystery note-taker. She was walking towards him with her palms turned up, her body language crying, 'What did I *do*?' He raised his chin and pinched the skin of his neck. His gaze travelled over her shoulder to me.

Mandy whipped round and saw me watching. 'What are *you* looking at?'

'Dunno,' I said, 'the label fell off.' It was a pat response, a playground taunt. All the same, it seemed to hurt her deeply. She shook her mane of hair and forced off a pout. For a second, the game came to life again without us.

'I hate you,' she whispered.

'With knobs on,' I said.

'MILLER, WAKE UP!' Mr Crozier bellowed, as the ball struck my heels and bounced out of play. The man in the sheepskin jacket smiled. He slid his pencil into the spine of his notebook. A sign, perhaps, that the county team would not be requiring my services this year.

The needle really went in after that. Every

nudge, every tap, every break in the play seemed to revolve around Mandy and me. We sparred, we bickered, we goaded, we glared. After I'd scythed her down one time we put our foreheads together like rutting deer. The referee booked me for dangerous play and gave Mandy her final, *final* warning. As the pressure built up, Hywel went for the kill. He'd been taunting Mandy non-stop throughout the half, and now the remarks got really cruel: *'Oi, your bum looks big in those shorts . . . Shouldn't you be at home doing the ironing or something? . . . You've got great cow's eyes – moo for us, go on.'*

And she was cracking, getting careless, making mistakes. She committed silly fouls, sliced passes into touch. One soft header back to her keeper left Ryan with a glorious scoring chance. He panicked and put his shot wide of the post. Bushloe High School breathed again.

But in the seventy-fifth minute their luck ran out. A simple through-ball finally broke the deadlock. Scott saw the opening and put me clear. No offside. Straight run on goal. The keeper was swiftly off his line, but showing too much of his left-hand upright. I steadied myself to curl the ball past him. *Gloop.* No go. It caught in a divot. I cancelled the shot and switched the ball left. The keeper, unbalanced, dropped to his knees. Sweet:

I'd fluked him the perfect dummy. As he flapped like a sea lion, I steered the ball round him. But again the conditions came to his rescue. The mud had tarred my boots so much I had to squelch my way into a shooting position. In that extra half-second he doubled back and lunged. He flashed out a hand and hooked my ankle. One moment I was looking at an open goal, the next I was eating Bushloe dirt.

The referee had no option: penalty.

Billy, on a hat-trick, begged to take it. Two sharp words from Scott squashed that. He handed me the ball. 'Make certain,' he whispered. I cleaned the ball and laid it on the penalty spot.

On the walk back I focused my mind. I pushed aside any thoughts about Billy or any misplaced loyalties to Mandy. Now it was me and the shark-toothed keeper, and all those years of practice on the garage. I breathed deeply and waited for the referee's signal. He whistled once, but not to me. Mandy was talking rapidly to the keeper, giving him advice by the look of things. But what could she tell him? She'd never even seen me take a penalty. I frowned and glanced at the referee again. In the distance, beyond him, a sheepskin jacket blurred into view. Was *that* how she knew? Tipped off? By a scout?

The referee blew. I started my run. I could go

left. I favoured right. One step from impact, I made my decision: I hit the ball straight. I figured if the keeper was going to dive, the best way to goal was plumb down the middle.

But the keeper didn't move. Maybe he was scared or maybe he was brave – or maybe he'd just had good advice. It didn't matter. The result was the same. I struck the ball so cleanly and hard that he barely had time to protect himself. He covered his face and *wham!* the ball cannoned down off his forearms, splatting back into the six-yard box. The mud killed the pace and the spin in one, setting me up for another snap shot. I needed two strides. I only managed one. As I steadied myself to squeeze the trigger, a hand whacked into the middle of my back, sending me flying to the ground once more. Feet tangled with my legs. Boots thudded round my ears. Then the ball was being struck, and there were whoops of joy.

Scott was the first one to me. 'You all right?' he panted, sliding on his knees. 'Billy scored. We're level. Danny, what's the matter?'

I rolled onto my back, my face contorting. 'It hurts,' I said. I put my hand on my groin.

'Oh no,' breathed Scott. 'Sir! Danny's injured.'

The referee bent over me. 'What is it, lad? Winded?'

'Pulled muscle,' said Scott as a crowd began to gather.

'Can you stand?' asked the ref.

'Don't know,' I squeaked.

Then another voice drifted into the scene. 'Shift! Come on. Get out of the way! Move!' And Mandy bustled through the press of bodies. She kneeled down beside me and gripped my hand.

'What are you doing?' said Scott. 'He's hurt. Get off him.'

'Shut up,' she said. 'It might be his appendix.'

'*Appendix?*' a dozen voices echoed.

'It grumbles,' said Mandy.

'Eh?' said Scott, and he tilted his head in the region of my groin like a cowboy listening for distant Indians.

At last, the teachers descended. Same questions. Some prodding. Much confusion. No-one seemed quite sure what to do. Then the man in the sheep-skin jacket turned up.

He crouched down and said, 'If a doctor has told him his appendix is grumbling, we can't afford to take any risks. This boy should go to a hospital, now. I can take him in my car, but someone he knows really ought to be with him.' He looked at Mr Crozier, who frowned in thought.

'I can't leave the team,' he said.

'And I can't abandon the match,' said the ref. 'Not at such a crucial stage.'

'And I can't stay long at the hospital,' said the man, easing me into a sitting position.

For a moment there was stalemate. Then Mandy stood up. 'I'll go,' she announced.

'You?' sneered Billy.

Mandy put her hands on her hips and said, 'Yeah. You got a problem with that?'

'But you don't know him,' said Hywel.

'I do,' said Mandy, with a flick of her hair. 'I'm his girlfriend. So there.'

Girlfriend? The word rattled wildly round the teams.

'Yeah, that makes sense,' Scott muttered, flicking a piece of mud off his shirt.

But the general tone was one of disbelief. Billy didn't mince his words too much. 'She's mental,' he said, gobbing on the pitch.

'Oh, yeah?' said Mandy, closing on him. 'And who was the one who just pushed him in the back? Some mate *you* are. At least I care what happens to him.'

'Mandy, give it up,' said the man in the jacket. He spoke with authority, like another teacher. He *knew* her, then? I looked him in the eye.

'I'm going to lift you,' he said, giving nothing away. He crooked my knees and raised me up. As the ref and Mr Crozier came to assist, the spat between Mandy and Billy grew worse.

'You're a load of rubbish, you are,' sneered Billy, almost starting a mass kerfuffle.

The Bushloe teacher called for order. He looked sternly at Mandy and said, 'Mandy, calm down and act sensibly, will you? You can't go to the hospital, you're still in the match.'

Mandy took several glances from her mates. Despite the warnings, she turned again on Billy. 'Tell me I'm rubbish again, I dare you.'

'You're rubbish,' he said.

And she punched him in the mouth.

'Jesus wept,' Mr Crozier said.

Hywel whistled softly and stood back a pace.

The referee sighed and produced a red card.

'Nice one,' said Scott, with a nod of admiration.

Mandy slipped off her captain's armband, threw it to Jezza and shook Scott's hand. 'Cheers. Have a good rest-of-game.'

The man in the jacket gave a shake of his head. He called to her to follow and carried me away.

'Bye, guys,' she said.

'Bye,' they said with a sigh of resignation. I had the feeling that nothing Mandy ever did surprised them.

Before she left, she paused over Billy. 'Funny, I never knew ducks had teeth.'

'*Pff off*,' he said, spitting one out.

Mandy showed him a finger and marched off the pitch.

And I couldn't help thinking that Billy deserved it.

INJURY TIME

They put me in the back of a large white car that had Swansea City stickers on the side and rear windows. Mandy draped a blanket round my shoulders then slid in beside me and belted me in. 'Is it bad?' she asked, nodding at my groin. There was studious concern in her bright blue eyes. 'Would rubbing it help?'

'No,' I said, and covered myself.

She snorted inwardly and let her eyes roll. 'Danny, I wasn't going to touch you up. It's a bit early in our relationship for that.'

'I think we'll let the doctors do the touching,' said the man. He started the car and joined the stream of traffic on the Cottersthorpe Road. 'Shouldn't take us long to reach the hospital. I'll ring your parents as soon as we get there, Danny. Just hang on. You're going to be fine.'

I looked at Mandy. She grinned right back. 'Thanks,' I said – to the man, not her. 'Excuse me, can I ask you something?'

'Sure, go ahead.'

'Who – who *are* you?'

Mandy wrinkled her nose. 'Who do you think he is?'

I shook my head. I was totally confused. 'Dunno. Scott saw you taking notes. We found a notebook after the game last week. We thought – you know – you might be a scout.'

Mandy hooted with laughter. 'He's my dad,' she said. 'He comes to support me, when he can take the time off work.'

Mr Woodruff smiled through his rear-view mirror. 'I am a scout of sorts,' he said. 'I don't just go to watch Dean or Mandy. During cup runs, I make notes about Bushloe's opponents.'

'Then he tells us who to watch out for,' said Mandy, rubbing a spear of dirt off her thigh. 'I was going to mark you originally, you know. But when Ian St Clair – he's our posh centre-half – got bugged with flu we decided I should play a free role instead. Versatile, aren't I?'

I nodded, thinking back to the book. Now I understood about the circled letters, 'Man' and 'ISC', and also how they knew about the free kicks and penalties. And Billy, of course. They knew lots about Billy. I sank down, letting my head clonk the window.

'Careful,' said Mandy. 'What's the matter?'

'Nothing,' I sulked, drawing up into a huddle. But I couldn't help adding, 'Bet you think I'm a right dork, don't you?'

'What about? The letter?'

I winced and looked away.

'It's OK,' she chirped. 'Didn't matter in the end. Dad sussed your mate was a diver all along.'

'Billy isn't my mate, not now,' I said glumly. 'And *I* didn't know your dad had been to watch us. Or that you—'

'What?' she said with an innocent shrug.

I thought it was perfectly obvious. 'You could have *told* me you weren't Adam.'

'Do I look like an Adam?' she said, a bit tautly, flicking her hair with the back of one hand. 'Adam's a *boy*. He's eight, and a pest. Actually, you might be pleased to know he's named his rubber duck Willowbrook after you.'

Even Mr Woodruff smiled at that.

I used silence and a scowl to show my indignation, but Mandy wouldn't let up. 'Anyway, I gave you loads of clues. I would have told you the truth that day at school if you hadn't tried to run me over with your bike.'

'I *didn't*.'

'So did.'

'It was an accident.'

'Puh.'

At this point Mr Woodruff intervened. 'Mandy, back off. You know the boy's hurt.' Before she could answer back he spoke to me again. 'Try not to feel hard done by, Danny. A lot of people are surprised to see Mandy playing football, especially competitive football. You wouldn't be the first to be caught off-balance.'

Which was a quaint way of putting it, I thought.

'Dad taught me everything I know,' said Mandy. 'We love footie, don't we, Dad?'

'Eat it, sleep it, breathe it,' he said, easing the car through a gap in the traffic. 'I was taking her to City's games – Swansea, where we come from – before she could walk, never mind kick.'

'Dad had trials with City,' she beamed. 'He could have been a pro, but he did his Achilles. I'm following in his footsteps.'

'How?' I said.

'Meaning?' she snapped.

Meaning, she couldn't play for Swansea City. That had to be obvious, even to her. But I knew right away I'd touched a nerve. She had sat up, straining against her seatbelt, her mouth drawn into a tight, firm line. I looked to her dad for manly support. But for once Mr Woodruff wasn't going to help. He was watching the lights and awaiting my response. Unsure of my ground, I tried to answer safely. 'It's just . . . you know.'

'Spit it out,' she said.

I shook my head. She'd done a pretty neat job of decking Billy. I didn't want to be next on the list.

'OK,' she said, 'I'll say it for you.' She posed with her hands held primly in her lap. 'I can't follow Dad because I'm a *girl*; a precious little princess, too dainty to play with the big, rough boys.' She cocked her head and fluttered her impressive eyelashes at me.

Thankfully, her dad chipped in with a comment. 'I don't think the Schools Football Association will think of you as "dainty" from now on, miss, not after what you did to Danny's striker.'

'He asked for it,' she carped. 'Did you see what he did for their second goal?'

'That's neither here nor there,' said Mr Woodruff. 'I've told you before: no matter how much someone taunts or intimidates, you never, ever, rise to their bait. Remember the George Best rule: if someone fouls you – or in this case tricks you – you humiliate them with your skill, not by knocking out their teeth.'

'I wanted to be with Danny,' she said, touching me gently on the arm.

'But that's stupid,' I told her.

'Oh, thanks a bunch!'

'But it is. If you win, you'll miss the final.' A sending-off carried a two-match suspension. Even a dummy like Billy knew that.

She folded her arms and went into a huff.

'Mandy, tell him the rest,' said her dad.

'You tell him,' she sulked.

Mr Woodruff sighed. 'I'm afraid it won't matter if they win or lose, Danny. There won't be any final for Bushloe now. Once that referee's report goes in, Mandy will be banned from playing for the team and the school will be disqualified from the competition.'

'Why?' I grimaced, pressing into my pain. I looked at Mandy, but she sniffed and turned away.

Mr Woodruff flicked his indicator on and nosed the car into the hospital grounds. 'Girls above the age of eleven are not allowed to play in a team with boys. There are some exceptions, for private clubs, but at school it's still forbidden.'

There was a pause, interrupted by the hiccup of road humps. 'Not allowed?' I said. 'You mean you cheated?'

228

'Excuse *me*?!' Mandy hooted, doing duck impressions.

Mr Woodruff shushed her and took up the argument. 'Technically, Bushloe have cheated,' he agreed. 'The difference being that, unlike your striker, there was no outright malice intended. We didn't play Mandy to try to be sneaky, we were hoping to draw some attention to her plight.'

'What does that mean?' I asked.

Mandy groaned and clawed her face. 'Oh, why are lads so *thick*?' She turned in her seat to lecture me again. 'When you're a girl and you're dead good at football, who are you s'posed to play with, eh? And before you say "Other girls," soppy, soppy, soppy, there aren't enough "other girls" to make up a team at Bushloe. If I was at Willowbrook, what would *you* do?'

'Dunno. Let you play, I 'spose.'

'S'pose!' She nearly burst out of her seatbelt. 'You'd pick me *first* if we were choosing teams for a kickabout in the yard.'

'But that's different. That's not proper football. If you're not allowed to play, then—'

'Danny, it's just a *rule*,' she cut in. 'And the lads in my team, they don't mind. They're dead pleased I play for the school. We're ten times better with me in the side, like Willowbrook are when you're with them. They all took a vote with Mr

Conway, our teacher. They said they'd support me, even though they knew that when someone made a fuss we'd be dumped from the Cup.'

'But what's the point of that?'

'Publicity, dummy. We wanted it to get in the local papers – and on the Schools' internet site. Then someone might change the rules.'

'But you'd be totally gutted if you won the Cup and then had to give it back – you'd lose your medal too.'

Mandy gave an indifferent shrug. 'Which would you rather: to be knocked out six–nil in the first round or have the thrill of making it to the final?'

Cup fever. She had a point.

'To be perfectly honest,' Mr Woodruff put in, 'I'm amazed we've come as far as we have. We were hoping to go all the way, of course, but Mandy scuppered that when she threw that punch. Instead of courting a bit of publicity, she's now going to attract a heap of notoriety. She does have to work on that temper of hers.'

'Dad!' she protested.

'Another time. We're here.'

We had pulled up next to a red-brick building fronted by a foyer of glass-panelled doors. The words ACCIDENT AND EMERGENCY were written in the glass. Ambulances waited in marked yellow areas. As Mandy and her dad got out of the car I saw someone in plaster being helped into a wheel-chair. I suddenly felt sick and weak inside. It didn't help when Mandy said, 'Shall I grab a trolley thing for Danny, Dad?'

'Mandy, we're not at the supermarket,' he said. 'I'll carry Danny. You go on ahead.' He opened my door and lifted me into his arms again.

The doors of the foyer swished open in wel-come. That hospital smell rushed into my nose. 'Make way!' shouted Mandy, waving her arms. The clack of her studs on the polished cream floors drew glances from people on the rows of orange chairs. A nurse in a dark blue uniform came over. She frowned at Mandy, then spoke to her dad. 'Has he broken something?'

'His appendix,' said Mandy. 'Five minutes from time. It wasn't me. The duck did him in. Will you have to operate?'

The nurse raised an eyebrow and turned to Mr Woodruff. 'Let's get him to reception. Are you his father?'

'I'm his girlfriend,' said Mandy. 'I'm here to look after him.' (From the seats, I thought I heard someone say, *'Aah.'*)

Mr Woodruff was less considerate. 'Mandy, this

is important, be quiet.' Then, to the nurse, 'No, no relation. And we haven't had a chance yet to contact his parents.'

The nurse nodded and rested a hand on my arm. 'Do you know your telephone number, luvvie?'

'Yes,' I said, beginning to shake. 'Please . . . ?'

She leaned in. 'Yes? What is it?'

'Please, I want my mum,' I whispered.

FINAL ANALYSIS

They told me I needed keyhole surgery.

'Where's his keyhole?' asked Mandy.

The doctor laughed. Alice slapped a hand against her forehead.

Mum said, 'You really don't have to stay, you know, Mandy.' She glanced rather pointedly at the clock.

Mandy smiled and said, 'Just another five minutes,' which had been her line for the last forty-five. 'Please may I speak to Danny alone?'

'I'm not dying,' I said, 'only lying on a couch.'

The doctor, an Asian man in a turban, clapped his knees and stood up, grinning. 'Five minutes, no more.' He spread five fingers. 'We'll be taking him down to a ward after that. Only family allowed in there.' (Alice looked at Mandy and grinned rather smugly.) 'No filthy shorts or unhygienic muddiness.' He pointed to the wedges of dirt on the floor, the product of Mandy's drying boots.

'We'll go and get a coffee from the drinks machine,' said Mum. She gave Mandy a sort of knowing look, squeezed my ankle and left with the doctor. Half a second later her hand came through the curtains and yanked Alice off her stool and out of sight.

Mandy lifted her shoulders and grinned. 'Smart. An operation. Think they'll let you keep the bits?'

'Do you mind?' I was nervous enough as it was.

'Cheer up,' she said. 'At least you won the game.'

On penalties. Six–five. It had gone to sudden death. Shortly before he'd had to leave, Mr Woodruff had phoned Mr Conway for us. 'Guess who got the winner?' he'd asked. We didn't need to guess. Rhubarb Billy: the four-goal 'hero'. Whoever said crime doesn't pay was wrong.

'It was a stupid game,' I muttered.

Mandy bobbed her head. 'Shall I tell you something?'

'What?'

'Eight out of ten people would prefer their team to play fairly, rather than win. I read that in the paper yesterday.'

'So?'

She popped her shoulders. 'Maybe Billy and Hywel were the two who said . . .' She stopped and crunkled her lip. 'Yeah, OK, it was a stupid game. Still, it brought us together, didn't it?'

I rolled my eyes and looked at her. She gulped and I knew the wrong words from me then would probably send her, tearful, for the exit. 'Why did you do it?' I asked. 'Say all that stuff about being my girlfriend? On the pitch, you said you hated me.'

''Course I don't hate you,' she said, squeezing up. 'It's just . . . I dunno. You wouldn't understand. It's . . .'

'A girl thing?' I said.

Her face widened in surprise. 'Aah, bless. You *do* understand.'

'Marcia taught me.'

'Oh,' she said, and looked at her knees.

'I'm not going with her, honest. We're only mates. It was Mum who made me invite her for tea.'

'Huh,' went a voice outside the curtains.

'Alice, go away or you're dead!' I barked. I

looked back at Mandy. 'She fancies Eddie Newton, Scott's older brother.'

'Who, Alice?'

'No, *Marcia*. She said we weren't . . . I mean, that you were . . . She said, y'know, I should *talk* to you. On the phone. I did *try*.'

She pushed her hands between her thighs and gave a rueful smile. 'I know. Bip, bip. I was mad at you then. Dead jealous, I s'pose – but I'm listening now.'

I looked her slowly up and down. Mandy Woodruff, the Bushloe superstar. She was covered in mud, socks bunching round her ankles, paw prints on her shirt, hair like a nest of stretched wire wool. Marcia Williams she certainly wasn't. But I liked her exactly the way she was, and the words, when they came, were easier than I'd thought. 'Do you wanna come and play footie on the park, with me and Scott?'

'Yeah,' she said, nodding twice as long as she needed to. 'That'd be really tidy. Course, we don't have to play football *all* the time, do we?'

Before I could ask what else she had in mind, the curtains swished and Mum and Alice came back.

Mandy sprang to her feet. 'Will you call me?' she asked.

Alice turned to Mum. 'She's not coming for tea, is she?'

Mum opened her handbag for something to do. Alice clucked and turned away in disgust.

Grinning, Mandy gave her a pat on the head. 'Gonna kiss your brother goodbye now, OK?'

The handbag snapped shut. 'Well, I don't think—'

But Mandy had landed it before Mum could finish. One quick peck and then she backed off. 'Get better,' she said. 'You'll be needed for the final. Bye, Alice. Bye, Mrs Miller. Oh, I forgot to ask Dad for some bus fare. I don't suppose you could lend me some, could you?'

Mum gave her enough for a taxi and sent her packing. And that was the last I would see of her, until my operation was over.

Although, I did . . . well . . . *dream* about her. When the doctor came to anaesthetize me, he injected something into the back of my hand and asked me to count from five to zero. 'Or,' he said, winking, 'if maths isn't your strong point, imagine yourself on the football pitch, running forward on goal, looking certain to score . . .'

And the next thing I knew I was flat on my face, hacked down from behind, slithering in mud. I heard the peep of a whistle and turned to the ref – and who should it be but Mandy Woodruff.

'Penalty?' I asked.

She put her nose in the air. 'I'm booking you for

taking a dive,' she said. 'Flagrant abuse of law ninety-nine.'

'Ninety-nine?' I queried. 'There aren't that many!'

'Want me to spell it out for you, Miller?'

'Yes, I do, *actually*,' I huffed.

She scratched three letters on her yellow card.

'FFM? What's that mean?' I said.

She flicked the card in the air and grinned. 'It's a boy thing,' she said. 'It's called Falling For Mandy.'